ASH

Jagged Edge

Series #5

A.L. Long

Copyright © 2017 A.L. Long
Ash: Jagged Edge Series #5

Interior edited by H. Elaine Roughton
Cover design by Laura Sanches

ASIN: B06XK96RSZ
ISBN: 9781544829012

This book is intended for mature audiences only

Acknowledgment

To my husband of many wonderful years, who has been so supportive of my writing. If it weren't for him my dream of writing would have never been fulfilled. I love you, sweetheart. And to my family, whom I also love dearly. Through their love and support, I can continue my passion for writing.

To the many readers, who took a chance on me and purchased my books. I hope that I can continue to fill your hearts with the passion I have grown to love.

Table of Contents

CHAPTER ONE

Ash

The best thing about having a day off is that I get to do what I love. Living out in the country has taught me how to really appreciate life and what I have. I know my grandparents didn't have it easy when raising me. Losing the only daughter they had to some stupid disease that I can't even pronounce couldn't have been easy on them. I could only remember bits and pieces of my childhood with her. Gramps and Granny raised me from the age of five. I often asked them about her, but I think it may have been too hard on them. Mostly they just told me that I was loved. Never knew my dad. I guess Mom got pregnant young and he pretty much disappeared.

Being their only grandson, they left this place to me. As much as I wanted to re-enlist after my eight-year term in the military, my home was here. This place meant a lot to them and I wasn't about to let it go to shit. So here I was, chilling on the front patio, drinking my brew and enjoying life.

At least I had my piece of solitude. Well, almost, until I recognized the black Camaro driving up the road. I could spot Peter's car a mile away. Working for Jagged Edge Security was never boring. Never knew what was going to happen, even on your day off.

I finished the last of my beer and began heading over to where Peter parked his car. I could see that Lou Gainer was riding shotgun. It was very rare that Peter would come all the way out here for just a friendly visit. I knew something must be up, and the minute he and Lou opened their doors, my suspicions were spot on. Their body movements couldn't have been more tense.

Looking over to Peter and then to Lou, I asked curiously, "What brings you guys out here?" knowing something was up with the two of them.

"Geez, Ash, you need to learn how to mellow out," Lou said, placing his hand on my shoulder.

"Normally when you guys pay a visit, you call first. Seeing how you didn't, I get this funny feeling this isn't a social call."

"Well, it is, sort of. How about a brew and we can discuss?" Peter asked.

Heading back to the house, Peter and Lou took their seat at the breakfast bar, while I went to the fridge for the beer. Unable to contain my curiosity, I handed them each a brew and asked, "So what's up?"

"So, you know that Sly and Nikki bought that new house and are planning on getting married next month," Peter pointed out.

"Yeah, so?" I replied.

"Well, me and the guys thought it would be nice to throw Sly a bachelor party," Peter began. "It doesn't have to be anything big or fancy. All of us, a few brews, not much."

"Okay, sounds good, but somehow I get the feeling that isn't all," I responded.

"The thing is, we thought it would be nice to have it here. You have all this room and since your place is by far the biggest, if anyone drank too much they would be able to crash here," Lou added.

As I looked over to the guys, it seemed like having a bachelor party here at the ranch had to do with a lot more than the sleeping arrangements. "Why do I get the feeling that there is more to this than just the party? Spill."

"Okay, okay. Me and the guys thought that maybe you would be willing to let us hire a couple of strippers, and if need be, they could stay here as well," Lou replied hesitantly, like he knew exactly what I was going to say.

"You know what, I think the stripper thing would be fun, but instead of allowing them to stay here, how about I arrange for their transportation back to the city. I think the last thing we need is for the girls to stop by and find a couple of strippers sleeping in the house. Not to say that they would ever show up, but just to keep it safe for you guys."

After arguing back and forth with Lou, he finally agreed that my suggestion was a better one than what he had planned, thanks to Peter swaying his decision. I know that Lou had a good heart, but sometimes he had a tendency not to think things through. One thing I did have to say for him, I would trust him with my life.

After we finished our beers, the guys left and I thought it would be nice to take a little walk. My grandpa and I use to take daily walks up the road when I was younger. He even coaxed me into going with him to the pond by convincing me that I needed to keep an eye out for snakes. His excuse was that his eyesight wasn't what it used to be. I knew that was a bunch of BS. I think more than anything, it was for the company.

Slipping on my shoes, I headed out the front door. The day couldn't have been any better. The weather was perfect for walking. Not too warm and not too cold. There wasn't even a cloud in the sky. It was strange how different the country was from the city. Everything was so much clearer. Even the birds singing could be heard crystal clear.

Breathing in the clean air, I looked around, thinking how blessed I was to have all of this. The circumstances that got me to this point were not what I wanted to remember, but I think my grandparents would have been proud of me, knowing that their property was being well cared for.

Lost in my thoughts, I heard a scream from up the road that sounded like a woman. Jogging in that direction, I spotted a young woman jumping up and down while holding her hand close to her body. Based on the hammer on the ground, my guess was that she missed the nail and was fighting off the pain from hitting her finger instead.

As I got closer to her, her eyes turned my way and I was hit with the most magnificent shade of green that I had ever seen. With her lips wrapped around her thumb, all I could think about was how gorgeous those lips were. My eyes were so completely fixed on her sucking away on her finger that I didn't hear a word she said.

"Can you hammer in a nail?" she asked softly as she pulled her thumb from her mouth, and my thoughts settled back to reality.

Picking up the hammer from the ground, I looked down at it and then to her. "I've pounded a few nails in my day. Looks like you could use a hand."

"Could I ever. My mom warned me about this place, said that I was too much of a city girl," she confessed.

I couldn't care less what kind of a girl she was; country, city, it didn't matter. All I knew was she was gorgeous and I couldn't keep my eyes off of her. The way her hair draped down her back like silk had me wanting to run my fingers through it. And, my God, those sassy shorts with the lace around the hem. Daisy Duke, watch out.

Moving the ladder out of the way that she had to use, since she was at least a good eight inches shorter than me, I straightened out the crooked nail and began pounding on the head with the hammer until it was flush with the wood trim. Satisfied, I handed the hammer back to her. Looking down at her, I couldn't help but stare at her. There was something in those eyes that kept me hypnotized. It was only after I heard her clear her throat that the spell was broken.

"I'm Juliette, by the way, but you can call me Jules. Thanks for your help," she said as I watched the words leave her mouth.

Tucking my hands in my pockets, I looked over to the road. "So, you just moved into this place?" I questioned.

"Yeah. Didn't know what I was getting myself into, though. I'm afraid there's a lot of work to be done. More than I realized," she confessed.

"Well, if you need help... I mean with this place, I only live a mile up the road."

"That's really nice of you. I'll keep that in mind. I should really get back to work. Thanks for the help," she said, opening the screen door.

Just like that she was out of sight. Turning on my heels, I stepped off the porch and headed back to my place. As I was walking a thought came to mind. I drove past this house at least twice a day and I never noticed that there was a for sale sign in the yard. The only thing that I could come up was that it must have been sold before the realtor had a chance to put a sign up. No matter, at least I now had a neighbor, and a gorgeous one at that. She was definitely someone that I would be borrowing a cup of sugar from.

~****~

When I got back to the house, I decided to find out more about my new neighbor. One thing about being in the security business, I had ways of finding out information on a person that the average Joe didn't. Walking to my office, just off of the kitchen, I took a seat at my desk and flipped up the top of my laptop and waited for it to come to life. Opening the search database, I plugged in the address of the house that was now occupied by the sexy green-eyed bombshell that had my dick rock-hard.

One thing I did know about the place was that the old couple that had once owned it moved to Nebraska where their daughter lived. They were getting up in age and their daughter didn't feel comfortable leaving them out here alone. They were the nicest couple, but a little on the strange side. I don't think there was anything they got rid of. The property looked more like a junkyard than anything else. I could only imagine how their daughter felt when it came time to move them and all their stuff.

Pulling up the property, I could see that the title to the property had changed over to Miss Juliette Daniels about a month ago. Not sure what her relationship was to the old couple. Maybe she was their granddaughter. or maybe just an interested buyer. It really didn't matter; at least I had a last name to go with that pretty face.

Switching applications, I typed in her name to see what would come up. There wasn't much on her once the information began downloading. She was born in Mountain Brook, Alabama, with a population of around 20,000. The only living parent was Carol Daniels, who still lived in the small town. She was twenty-three and currently attending The City College. She seemed like she had everything together. She was a good girl. Not even so much as a parking ticket on her.

Shutting down my computer, I gazed out the window across the road that led to her home. There was something about her that made me want to find out more. I had all the information I needed for now, at least what was on paper. Now, all I wanted was to really get to know her. Find out what she liked and what she didn't. Really get to know her.

CHAPTER TWO

Juliette

It was hard to believe that I was finally on my own and out of the city. Even though my mom warned me about this place, I couldn't pass it up; it was a steal. At least that was what I thought until I started living here. The amount of work this place needed was way beyond anything I would be able to do myself. I was a girly girl, and doing handy work just wasn't in my genes. Unfortunately, I needed to learn quickly. There was no way I could afford to hire a man to do the work. Going to college part-time and only working nights didn't leave me with the cash flow I needed. Getting a degree was the most important thing to me. All I wanted to do was find a good job, a respectable one that my mom would be proud of.

Making a list of what I thought I would need to get this place in shape, I decided that I had better get a move on if I was going to anything done. Grabbing my purse, I checked to make sure I had my I.D., cash, and my handy Visa card, even though I knew I was pretty close to maxing

17

out the balance. Hopefully this new job would get me out of debt. I knew one thing for sure: being given this house was a godsend no matter the repairs that needed to be done. I would much rather put money into something that was mine than spend the money on rent.

As I grabbed my purse, my cell began to ring. Looking down at the screen, I could see that it was my mom. "Hey, Mom," I said.

"Hey, sweetheart. I just wanted to check on you and see how the house was coming along," she replied.

"It's getting there. Little by little," I answered

"So how about summer? You still planning on staying there?"

"I have so much to do here, Mom. I really would love to come home for a bit, but this is really important to me," I said, knowing that wasn't the only reason.

"Well, if you change your mind, let me know."

Ending the call, I headed out. Looking at the old house, I glanced up at the nail the hot guy, who I guess I could consider my next-door neighbor, was so kind to help me with and smiled. He would definitely be a neighbor I'd want to get to know better, if only I could. Right now there were too many things I needed to work out first, and having another distraction was not in the mix.

Getting in my car, I turned the key, only the engine wouldn't start. This was not what I needed. I knew I should have traded off my yellow bomb when I had the chance, but paying my tuition seemed like a better choice at the time. Opening the door, I walked to the front of the car and lifted the hood. It seemed like the most natural thing to do, even though I had no idea what I was even looking for. Looking down at the engine, I took in a deep breath and scratched my head. Closing the hood, I looked down the road and decided my best option was to see if Mr. Hot to Trot could figure out what was wrong with my car.

Walking down the dirt road, I was thankful that at least it was a gorgeous day. The heat may have been a little much, but it didn't matter. I just slipped off my button-up shirt and wrapped it around my waist. It was about a mile later, just like he said, when a beautiful house came into

19

view. "Wow, this guy really takes care of this place," I said to myself.

Looking up at the large windows in the front that extended from the wood deck to almost the highest peak of the house, I wondered who cleaned them when they got dirty. As magnificent as it was, it just didn't seem practical, except maybe to showcase a fifteen-foot Christmas tree. I climbed the steps to where the front door was. The door was over-the-top gorgeous, with stained-glass windows and fancy brass handles on each side. Almost afraid to knock on the beautiful glass, I searched for the doorbell as an alternative. Every home should have one, I thought, but for some reason there wasn't one to be found. Tapping lightly on the glass, I could only hope that the gorgeous guy inside would be able to hear me.

When the door opened, he couldn't have been more gorgeous. The green-blue of his eyes seemed even more mesmerizing with the sun hitting them just right. And with the dark of his eyelashes surrounding them, I knew they broke plenty of hearts. Smiling up at him, I was at a loss for words. With a little chuckle and the cutest smile ever, he said curiously, "I was just thinking about you."

Little did he know that I was thinking about him as well. "I'm sorry to bother you, but my car doesn't seem to want to start, and I don't know anything about cars except where to put the gas."

"Let me get my shoes on and I'll check it out," he said.

I couldn't help but lower my eyes to his feet. If there was ever a man who could have the sexiest feet ever, it would have to be him. Realizing that I didn't even know his name, I asked abruptly, stopping him in his tracks. "What is your name? I mean, you never said."

"Ash," he replied.

A perfect name for a perfect man. "Nice to meet you, Ash," I said as he stepped to the side, gesturing for me to come inside.

I couldn't believe this place. Just the entrance alone was magnificent, with its high ceilings and skylights. I wondered what it looked like at night with the stars shining through the glass. Pulling me from my stupor, he said, "Make yourself at home. I'll be right back."

21

Nodding my head in agreement, I watched him leave the area before I began making myself comfortable. Wandering to my left, I stepped into the living area where the floor-to-ceiling windows were. I had to take back everything I said. The way the outside beamed though the glass, it was no wonder the larger windows were put in place. Looking around, I could see that there was also a fireplace. What an awesome room this would be to have family get-togethers.

Turning away from the window, I spotted the kitchen to my left. It was massive, just like the living area. There was a center island with a granite top and a matching counter behind it. All of the appliances were stainless steel, which made the kitchen very classy. Hearing footsteps behind me, I turned and said, "This place is amazing."

"I grew up here. My grandparents left this place to me when they passed. I've made a few upgrades over the years. Made it more me," Ash replied.

"I'll say. It is breathtaking."

"Come on. Let's see what's going on with your car."

When Ash took my hand and led me to a door in the kitchen, I was almost hesitant to go with him, but when I saw the steps leading to the garage, my mind was put at ease. Even though he seemed like a nice guy, it always seemed as though those were the type of guys a girl needed to be careful of.

Ash walked to the passenger side of his truck, opened the door, and made sure I got in safely. It took him a while to get in himself. My guess was that he was looking for tools, in case he needed them to fix my yellow bomb. My little Civic was something my mom bought for me on my eighteenth birthday. I thought I had died and gone to heaven when I got that little car. Now I wasn't so sure, hence the recent name I gave it. I think over the years I put more money into it than it was actually worth. I never had the heart to get rid of it. Plus, there was the fact I would never be able to afford a new one.

As Ash started the truck, the garage door began to open and he pulled out. It seemed kind of silly driving to my home, especially since I lived only a mile away. He only grabbed a handful of tools, so it wouldn't have been a problem to walk the short distance.

When we pulled up to my little house, my car looked pathetic against Ash's beautiful truck. The minute he looked over to me, I knew he was thinking the same thing. Before he could say anything, I said firmly, "It was a gift from my mom and I refuse to sell it."

With a half smile, he responded. "Jules, I don't think you would get anything for it. It looks like your car is on its last leg, or in this case, spark plug."

I watched Ash get out of the truck and walk to my car. Lifting the hood, I could tell that he was a little bit concerned given the way he was shaking his head. Opening my door, I got out and walked over to him. We were standing next to each other, side by side, looking at the engine. Ash still shook his head while I wondered what he was thinking. "When was the last time you had a tune-up?" he questioned.

Gazing down at the engine, I said in a soft voice, "The last time I had an oil change, which may have been about six months ago."

"Well, whoever checked it over should have suggested you have all of the wiring replaced. I will see what I can do, but I would definitely get them replaced."

24

I knew he was right. The yellow bomb was old and probably on its last leg, but it had been with me a long time and had gotten me out of a lot of predicaments. Making his way back to his truck, I watched him as he opened the door to the back seat and grabbed what few tools he had. When he came back, he began working on the engine. I had no idea what he was doing, but I was pretty sure he knew more about car engines than I did.

"Do you have your key?" he asked.

Reaching in my front pocket, I pulled out my key, which was attached to my lucky pink rabbit's foot. Handing it over to him, I watched him slide into the front seat of my car, having a little difficulty fitting his muscular body behind the wheel. When he was finally able to get seated, he turned the key in the ignition and the car began to sputter. With a few more pumps on the gas pedal, the engine started. I put my hands together and began clapping at the success he had.

Climbing out of the car as best he could, he looked down on me and said with concern, "I'm not sure how long it is going to stay started. I think I better follow you to the service station in case it dies on you."

"I wasn't planning on going to the station. I need to pick up some supplies for the house," I replied, matter-of-factly.

"This is more important, Jules. If you don't get it fixed, you could be left stranded," he said firmly.

"How am I supposed to get the things I need if my car is being serviced? It is the only means of transportation that I have." Maybe I could leave it to get serviced. I guess I could check into renting a car until it was done, but then I would be spending money that I didn't have.

"Okay, how about this? I will take you wherever you need to go. Based on the condition of your car, my guess would be that your car is going to be out of commission for at least a week," he offered with a half smile.

"You would be willing to do that for me?" I replied.

"Yeah."

I could have given Ash a hug, but instead I got in my car. I was thankful that he came by when he did earlier. If he hadn't been there to help me, I would have never known to walk to his house. Putting the car in reverse, I slowly back out of the driveway, careful not to run into Ash's truck. Heading down the road, I looked back in my review mirror to make sure that Ash was still behind me.

An hour later, we were leaving the service station with information I wasn't expecting to hear. The entire engine needed to be rewired. It was either that or purchase a new engine altogether. There was very little cost difference between the two, so I looked to Ash for advice. After paying up $1,200, I was buying a new engine for my car.

Our first stop would be the hardware store. I hoped that it carried everything I needed for the repairs to be done to the house. I needed to get some more nails, paint, a few two-by-fours, and some tape. This would at least be enough to get me started. Hopefully, this house wouldn't turn into a money pit and drain every last penny from my savings.

After I found everything I needed, Ash carried the items to his truck while I finished paying for them. As I opened the door to the truck, I noticed a man leaning up against a light pole across the street. It wouldn't have seemed unusual except he was dressed in a hoodie and it was at least ninety-five degrees outside. Not only was that strange, he was looking right at me. Climbing in, I buckled my seat beat and waited for Ash to get in. Seeing that he was settled, I looked out the back window to see that the creepy man was still leaning against the light pole watching us.

"What do you think that guy is waiting for?" I asked, trying to act like I was unaffected by the man's presence and the fact that he was watching us.

Looking out his side mirror, Ash turned the key in the ignition and said, "Beats me. Kind of creepy though."

It never occurred to me that Ash would actually drive over to where the guy was standing and confront him. Pulling up to the curb, Ash rolled down his window and asked bluntly, "Is there something you need?"

When the guy looked at Ash with a pissed-off look before he walked away, I thought for sure that Ash would jump out of his truck and find out what his problem was, but he didn't. He just shook his head and put the truck into drive and pulled away from the curb. All I knew was the guy looked creepy, and when he looked at Ash the way he did, there was something really off about him.

28

The drive back to my place was killing me with the silence between us. There was still something bothering me about the guy in town and I needed to vent my opinion. "What do you think that guy in town wanted?" I asked, gazing out the side window and then over to Ash.

"I don't know, but there was definitely something strange about him. He certainly wasn't from around here," Ash confessed.

"Personally, I think he may have been on something. Who in their right mind wears a hoodie in the middle of summer?" I replied.

"Does seem kind of strange."

When we got to the house, Ash began unloading the items from the back of the truck. Even though I would have been able to do it myself, I was glad that I didn't have to. Once he had everything inside the house, I thought for sure that he would be on his way, but he surprised me when he said, "I'll get started in the bathroom. I know how you women are."

Before I could protest, he was grabbing the two-by-fours and heading down the hallway to the bathroom. The way he moved around the house made me wonder if he had been in the place before. Moving in the other direction, I grabbed the new faucet hardware and headed to the kitchen. If Ash was willing to offer his help, who was I to stop him? It would certainly shorten the amount of time it would take to get this place in shape.

CHAPTER THREE

Ash

I knew the minute that Juliette spotted that guy across the street, she would think something was up with him. What she didn't realize was that I saw him before we got to the hardware store. He was also at the service station where we dropped off her car. I knew I should have approached him then, but I really didn't think anything of it at the time. I had a funny feeling there was more to this guy. I knew one thing for sure, the next time I laid eyes on him, he wouldn't be getting away so easy.

Focusing my thoughts back on the repairs I was working on in the bathroom, another thought came to me. *"What in the hell possessed Juliette to buy this place?"* I understood her wanting to have something of her own, but this was in no way worth keeping. From a distance it really didn't look that bad, but up close, it was an accident waiting to happen.

31

Finishing what I could in the bathroom, I headed to the kitchen to see if there was anything I could do to help Juliette with the faucet. Stopping just outside the doorway, I looked down to the floor and saw those gorgeous tan legs peeking out from under the sink while the rest of her body was resting inside the cabinet. She must have had her iPod going because she didn't even move when I called her name.

Walking over to where she was, I lowered my body to see if I could figure out what she was doing. The best I could see, she was trying to tighten the gooseneck part of the plumbing. It looked like she wasn't having any success, so I tapped her lightly on the leg to get her attention. Her head came up so quickly that she couldn't miss hitting her head on the opening of the cabinet. *"Dang, that's gotta hurt,"* I thought to myself as a screeching sound came from her pretty mouth.

"Shit, shit, shit!" she cried, rubbing the top of her head.

I couldn't help but laugh at the way she looked. It had to have been the cutest pout on a face I had ever seen. Helping her to her feet, I took the wrench from her hand and squeezed my upper body inside the small area. I guess I

32

shouldn't have laughed at her because the minute I turned the pipe, it split in half, causing water to gush out and burst the pipe wide open. I guess I deserved that.

With my upper body completely soaked, I pushed from the floor, knowing that Juliette was now laughing at me. At least it made her forget about the bump that was beginning to form on her forehead. Grabbing the nearest towel, I began wiping off the excess water. Getting as dry as I could get with the small dish towel, I looked over to Juliette and said, concerned, "You may want to put some ice on the bump."

"I'm good. What are we going to do about the sink?" she asked frantically.

"The first thing we need to do is turn the water off. It's too late to get another part, so we will need to do it in the morning."

"What am I supposed to do without water until tomorrow?" she huffed, throwing her hands up in the air.

"It's okay, Jules. You can stay the night with me. I have a guest room with an attached bathroom."

"I can't do that... This is just great. Not only do I not have a car, now I don't even have water, and I have to be to work in three hours."

The way she was pacing back and forth, you would have thought it was the end of the world for her. Stopping her from wearing down the flooring, I looked down at her and assured her that it would all work out. "Jules, you are making this more of a big deal than it needs to be. You can stay with me; shower and I will give you a ride to work. You can call me when you're off and I will be there to pick you up. Not a big deal."

"You would do all of that for me? You hardly know me."

"As I said, it's not a big deal. Get what you need and we can get out of here," I said, hoping that she would do as I asked and not stress about it.

Taking a seat on the couch, I waited for her to gather the things she needed. I was surprised that she accepted my offer. She was right about one thing, we hardly knew each other, but I could see a woman in need a mile away, and Juliette was definitely a woman in need. A faint ringing

34

interrupted my thoughts. I took my phone from my pocket and looked down at the screen. Swiping the accept button, I hesitantly said, "Hello." I wasn't sure who was on the other side, but I knew there was someone there. Before I could say another word, the caller hung up. You would have thought that I would have learned that unknown callers were just that, unknown.

Juliette entered the living room, packing a suitcase that was big enough to be considered more than for an overnight stay. I knew that girls had more necessities than just a change of clothes and a toothbrush, but by the way she was struggling with the case, it had to be packed plump full of who knew what.

Standing, I walked over to where she was and helped her with her suitcase. The minute I took it from her, it was no wonder she was having such a hard time. "Jesus, girl, what do you have in this thing?"

"Only the stuff I need," she replied with an annoyed expression.

"Okay, I guess I shouldn't have asked."

After locking up the house, we got into my truck and headed to my place. It was going to be strange having someone besides the guys stay the night at the house. It was also going to be hard to simmer down the things that I would love to do to this woman. I only prayed that she didn't have one of those sexy nighties that got a man all hard and shit.

When we reached the house, I pulled the truck forward and backed up into the garage. Satisfied that I was in far enough, I cut the engine and got out. Walking to the back of the truck, I opened the tailgate and grabbed Jules' suitcase. Still couldn't believe how heavy the dang thing was.

Heading inside, I led her to the guest bedroom. I hoped that it would be sufficient for her needs. Looking over my shoulder, I made sure that she was still following behind me. When we got to the room, I swung open the door and walked over to the bed, where I placed her suitcase. As I turned towards her, I could see that she approved of the accommodations, based on the look on her face.

"The bathroom is through there," I said as I pointed in the direction of the bathroom door.

"Great, thanks," she said with a beautiful grin.

36

"If you need anything, let me know. Steak okay?" I asked.

"Steak?"

"Yeah, for dinner. Do you like steak?" I replied.

"Steak is good." she confirmed.

"Great." I backed out of the room and left her to do her thing. Having her here was going to be hard. I had never wanted a woman as much as I wanted her at that moment, and the bulge in my jeans was confirmation of that. Closing the door, I headed to the kitchen to season some steaks. I wasn't even sure how she liked it cooked. If I had to guess, well done.

As I began preparing the meal, I could have sworn I heard something. Going to the living room, I waited for a moment to see if I could hear it again. Thinking I must be losing it, I went back to the kitchen to finish up. Right then, I actually did lose it. Standing in absolutely nothing was the most gorgeous body I had ever seen. She was perfect in every aspect. Her breasts were just the right size in comparison to the rest of her body, with her nipples standing at full attention; my guess was because of being wet and completely naked. The rest of her body was breathtaking, like God knew exactly what the body of a woman should look like. Pure perfection.

"Excuse me, but can I get a towel?" she asked, pulling me from the effect her beauty had on me.

Babbling incoherently, I said, "Umm, yeah," as I walked over to the soft blanket that was draped over the back of the couch. It was the only thing I could find in a hurry that still allowed me to keep my eyes fixated on her.

As she turned around I wrapped the blanket around her shoulders, allowing me to get a better look at her. One thing that I did notice was the tiny tattoo she had on her neck, just below her hairline. It was some sort of symbol with two S's. One was right side up and the other was connected at the bottom and upside down. Curious as to what it meant, I asked, "What does your tattoo mean?"

Taking hold of the blanket and pulling it tighter around her, she replied, "I need to get dressed," before walking away and heading back to her room.

I knew my mouth was wide open with awe. I could only imagine what she might have thought about the way I was looking at her. Trying to forget about how much of an ass I just made of myself, I went back to what I was doing and tried to forget about the whole thing. Yep, this was definitely going to take some doing on my part to tame down my desire to take her.

CHAPTER FOUR
Juliette

Finishing my wonderful shower, I looked everywhere for a towel, but there weren't any in the bathroom or the bedroom. The only option I had was to find Ash and ask him where they were. The look on his face was priceless. I had no idea that my nudity would have such a profound effect on him. I did have to admit it was kind of sweet the way he grabbed the blanket and draped it over me. The chance of him seeing my tattoo was something I forgot about. Having it for as long as I had, it was a part of me now, something that I would never be able to erase.

Looking at the time, I knew I had better hurry if I wanted to make it to work on time. At least that was what I called it. It was more like a living hell. The upside was that it allowed me to have my days so that I could finally make a home for myself. Tonight, as awful as it was going to be, would give me enough money to fix my car and buy the additional items for the house to finish the repairs.

Quickly getting dressed, I headed back to the kitchen where I knew Ash was. As I left my room, the smell of something wonderful filled the air. I wasn't sure how good of a cook he actually was, but whatever he was cooking smelled divine. The minute I got to the kitchen, I couldn't believe what I saw. The table was dressed like something you would see in a fancy restaurant, aside from the cloth napkins. Unable to understand what all the fuss was, I walked over to where Ash was standing, opening a bottle of wine.

"You do know that I have to be to work in less than two hours," I pointed out.

"I do, but steak always tastes better with red wine. And besides, one glass isn't going to hurt," he answered.

Taking a seat at the beautifully displayed table, I did my part and placed my napkin on my lap, and waited for Ash to bring the dinner he prepared to the table. I had to admit that the way the food looked on the plate, he was probably a better cook than I was. Waiting until he was settled in his chair, I picked up my glass of wine and proposed a toast. "Here is to a wonderful meal prepared by an amazing guy."

Nodding his head, his mouth angled into a breathtaking smile that made my body tingle. It was at that moment I could feel a slight wetness between my legs. I wondered how many other women melted whenever he smiled. Taking a bite of my steak, my lips wrapped around the fork, my taste buds were dancing with delight at the wonderful treat they were given.

"Oh, my God, Ash, this is amazing," I said with delight.

"I knew you would enjoy it. One of the many things I enjoy doing is cooking," he confessed.

"And what would be the other things you enjoy doing?" I asked.

"Aside from helping a beautiful woman in distress, I like fishing and camping, hanging out with the guys. What about you, what do you enjoy doing?"

I wasn't sure how to answer that. It had been so long since I had enjoyed anything. The last thing I remembered was hanging out with my friends at the swimming pool. I remember my mom telling me that one day I would be on the

Olympic team. If she knew what my life was now she would have a heart attack. As far as she knew I worked nights at a distribution center. If that wasn't a bad enough lie, I told her that I was a shift manager. It would kill her if she knew what I actually did at night.

"I guess that was too personal," Ash commented.

Looking up at him, I took my napkin from my lap and wiped it gracefully across my lips. "It's not that," I began, taking a breath. "I just can't remember the last time I enjoyed anything. Seems the only thing I have been doing lately is work. And everyone knows that work is very seldom enjoyable.

"So, what is it that you do?"

I knew sooner or later that question would be coming up. Lowering my head so that he wouldn't be able to read my face, I answered with a controlled voice, "I work at A&J Distribution center."

"Really! The one just outside of New York City?"

"Yeah, that's the one," I replied.

43

"I didn't think it was still open," Ash countered.

I was glad my head was lowered. If he had seen my reaction, he would have known that I was telling him a lie. As far as I knew it was still open, but I hadn't checked it out in a couple of months. I needed to say something. "Nah, they're just going through a transition. Anyway, I better finish getting ready."

Pushing from the table, I needed to get away from this conversation. The last thing I needed was to share too much information with him. The less he knew about me the better it would be. Dodging the bullet, I made it to my room. I had everything that I needed to take laid out on the bed. One thing about my so-called job, I was provided with nice things to wear. Placing the midnight blue beaded gown on top of my shoes and make-up case, I made sure not to get it wrinkled. I zipped up my bag and sat on the bed until I was ready to go. As I sat on the bed and waited, I must have pulled my phone out at least a dozen times to look at where I was supposed to go and the best route there from the distribution center. The only thing that I needed to worry about was what I was going to say to Ash if he was right about the center and it was closed.

Slinging my bag over my shoulder, I opened the door to my room and headed to the main part of the house. Entering the living room, Ash was sitting on the couch looking out the floor-to-ceiling windows. Placing my bag on the hard floor a little more forcefully than I needed to, I was able to at least get his attention. Walking over to him, I looked out the window and took in the beautiful sight. "No wonder you love it here. This view is amazing," I confessed.

"Yeah, my grandpa knew exactly what he was doing when he built this house forty-some years ago. With all the work I've done to this place, one thing I would never change is this magnificent view." Pausing a moment, he turned to me and asked, "Are you ready to go?"

Walking over to where I left my bag, I put it over my shoulder and followed Ash through the kitchen and down the stairs to his truck. As I got into the truck, it dawned on me that there was a transit stop just outside the city. If I could convince him to drop me off there, then he wouldn't go directly to the distribution center and see that it was closed. That was my only hope.

As we drove down the dirt road to the main road, my cell began to vibrate in my pocket. Pulling it free, I looked down at the screen and recognized the number right away. I knew I couldn't answer the call and chance him finding out who I was talking to. Instead, I sent a quick text and placed my phone back in my pocket. I was thankful that Ash didn't question who I was texting. Getting to the main road, I took a deep breath and said in no uncertain terms. "You can drop me off at the bus stop. It's not far from the distribution center. This way you don't have to drive all the way into the city."

"Don't be silly, Jules. I need to go to the shop anyway," Ash confessed.

"Shop?" I questioned.

"Yeah, I work for Jagged Edge Security and thought I would catch up on stuff while I waited for you to get off."

"But that won't be until early in the morning. I can take a cab or something back."

"No can do. Put this number in your phone. Call me when you're close to getting off and I will come get you.

I could feel my throat tighten as I took my cell from my pocket. The hole I was digging was getting bigger and bigger. There was no way out of this. As Ash rattled off his number, I entered it into my phone. When I finished with all seven numbers, I decided to look up A&J Distribution to see for sure what kind of pickle I was going to be in. When the link came up, I quickly clicked on it to find that I was saved. It appeared that someone had purchased the center about six months ago in a large takeover. I let out the breath I was holding and looked to the sky, thanking God for answering my prayer.

Finally getting to the distribution center after what seemed like the longest ride of my life, I reached for my bag, which I had placed in the back seat, and opened the door. Looking over to Ash before I closed the door, I asked, "Are you sure you don't mind picking me up? It could be later in the morning."

"Jules, I'm sure. Don't stress."

"Okay, I'll call you then."

Closing the door, I began walking to the front door at a turtle's pace, hoping that Ash would be out of sight before I darted in the other direction. When he was out of view, I made my way back to the main street, where I knew I could catch a transit bus into the city. It wasn't long until a bus showed up. Trying to calculate the time, I estimated that I would have about twenty minutes to get changed and ready for my job.

Sitting on the bus, I thought about what would happen tonight. Even though the money would be good, there was still that small chance that something could go wrong. I never knew what would happen or what my night would consist of. The way I was feeling, I hoped it wasn't going to be too extreme. Looking out the window, I waited for the bus to pull over to my stop before gathering my bag. Once I stepped off, I looked up at the Mandarin Oriental and took in its magnificence. This would be the first time I had ever been here, but from what I heard, a lot of diplomats stayed here.

Entering the big hotel, the first thing I needed to find was the restroom. No way did I need to be caught looking the way I did when my master showed up. Looking around the lobby area, I finally spotted the women's powder room. "Powder room" was something I hadn't normally seen. This place must be really upscale. Pushing open the door, an elderly lady was wiping down the counter with a white towel.

Looking over to me with a smile, she asked politely, "Is there anything I can help you with?"

Walking closer to her, I said softly, "Is there a place where I can change?"

This must have been some place. Never had I seen a bathroom attendant, at least that was what I guessed she was. With a smile still on her face, she held out her hand. I wasn't sure what she wanted so I placed my hand in hers. With her other hand, she covered her mouth as if embarrassed and said, "No, Miss. I meant to take your bag."

Pulling my hand from hers, I handed her my bag, feeling a bit like an idiot. I began to follow her until she stopped in front of a wooden door. Standing in front of the door, she set my bag on the floor, then reached inside the pocket of her crisp white apron and pulled out a set of keys. Opening the door, she picked up my bag and placed it on the small bench that was inside the room. I wasn't sure what she was expecting, but when she didn't move, I knew she was waiting for a tip. Unzipping my bag, I pulled a five dollar bill from my wallet and handed it to her. Before she could take it from my hand, I said to her firmly, "If you watch my bag and don't let anyone take it, I will triple that tip."

Nodding her head, she replied, "It would be my pleasure, Miss."

Letting go of the bill, I closed the door and unzipped my bag. Pulling out the dress I had carefully placed on the top, I shook out the wrinkles and slung it over the door until I was ready to put it on. I knew that this was an important night and I had to be on my best behavior if I wanted to get paid top dollar. Just like every other time, I knew the only way to get through this was to take my thoughts away from here to another place.

Slipping on my dress, I looked at myself in the full-length mirror to make sure nothing was hanging out that wasn't supposed to be. I had to admit I looked pretty good. Touching up my make-up with what I had packed in my bag, I was as ready as I would ever be to tackle what was in store for me.

Opening the door to the dressing room, I handed my bag over to the attendant and exited the powder room. No sooner than I opened the door, I heard his voice. "You look lovely, pet. Are you ready to play?"

CHAPTER FIVE

Ash

Despite dropping Juliette off at A&J Distribution, I was still not buying that she worked there. Driving around the block, I had to see for myself if what she said was actually true. Even though it looked to be in operation, I knew the minute I saw her that she was no more an employee there than I was her brother.

I stayed close to her until she hopped on the transit bus. You wouldn't think that a person could lose sight of a bus, but I did. I had no idea where it was headed or even its route. I wasn't even smart enough to get the number of the bus that was usually painted on the back in big black letters. Knowing that I had at least eight hours before she would be calling me to pick her up, I decided to head over to the shop and see if I could find out anything about the routes of the transit buses. If anything, at least I would be better prepared to follow where she would end up.

It was close to nine o'clock when I arrived at the shop. I knew that the guys left hours ago, giving me a chance to do some uninterrupted research. Opening the door to the shop, it didn't surprise me that Peter's office light was still on. Heading in that direction, I wondered what he was doing in the shop so late.

As I peeked around the corner, he looked to be heavy in thought, with his hands cupping his head. Knocking lightly on the door frame, I waited until his head lifted and he saw me. Walking into his office, I placed my hands on the back of the chair in front of his desk and asked hesitantly, "What's up, Peter? You're here late.

"You are going to find out soon enough. You might want to take a seat for this," he offered.

Walking around the chair, I sat down and waited for Peter to tell me what was on his mind. I wasn't sure how to read the expression he had on his face. It could have been a look of confusion, or maybe skepticism. Either way, Peter looked out of sorts.

"By the look on your face, you are having a hard time digesting whatever it is you have to say," I shared.

52

"After what I have to tell you, you are going to think the same thing," he started. "Do you remember the mission we had in Nicaragua?"

"Yeah, I remember. Even though I stayed behind, I remember the mission," I replied.

"Well, something has come up in the States; here, to be exact. And it gets even worse. I don't know all the specifics yet, but by the sound of it, it is pretty bad."

"No matter how bad it is, Peter, you know we are able to handle it. Jagged Edge Security always comes out on top."

Leaving Peter's office, I headed to the conference room to do a little research on another problem. One with a tight little ass and a drop-dead gorgeous body. Booting up the conference room laptop, I waited for it to come to life. Pulling up the Internet, I typed in 'MTA bus transit.' Just like that, the link I needed was at the top of the list. Clicking on the link, it led me to another link. I didn't realize that the bus transit had so many routes. Finding the one I needed, I clicked print and waited for the map to print.

The search took all of a few minutes, giving me plenty of time to do some more research on my gorgeous, but mysterious, neighbor. The one thing that bothered me the most was her tattoo. She was hesitant to let me know what it meant, so the best way for me to find out was to research it myself. As I typed in double S, images began to appear. Finding the one that looked exactly like Juliette's, I finally knew what it meant, *"Ownership."* My next search was going to be on Juliette. Since I now knew her last name, I typed Juliette Daniels in the search engine and waited for something to come up. Nothing of value showed, at least nothing that I didn't already know. Pulling up the data software, I knew it would give me more information than what I would get on the Internet. It was the best software out there to find out the truth about a person, past and present. I entered the needed information, most of which I guessed on, and hoped for the best. The program was going crazy when it finally stopped. There, plain as day, was a mug shot of my Juliette. She looked to be only in her teens in the picture, but it was most definitely her. What I couldn't understand was how someone that seemed so wholesome could have a police record. Scrolling down the page, I tried to find out more, but when I tried to click on the link to open the criminal record history, I kept getting, '**This page cannot be displayed**' in bold letters. There could only be one reason for this. All of her records were sealed and only a person with authorization could open them.

Closing the lid to the laptop, I began to wonder who this woman was that had me so interested. I knew no one had a perfect life and that everyone had skeletons in their closet, but I just couldn't let her unknown record go. It was going to eat at me until I found out the truth about Ms. Daniels. Heading back to Peter's office, hoping he was still around, I knew he would know of someone who could help.

Tapping on his door, I looked at him and said, "I need your help with something," as I walked in and took a seat in the chair in front of his desk.

"Shoot, bro," Peter answered, leaning back in his chair and placing his hands behind his head.

"Okay, so here's the deal," I began. "There is a new girl that moved into the old Willows place up the road from me. Anyway, I really like this girl, but something is off with her."

"Off, how?"

"Well, earlier tonight, I dropped her off at the A&J Distribution Center. She said she worked nights there. The thing is, I saw her walking away from the building and catching a bus. I tried following it, but I lost it."

"How could you lose a bus?" Peter chuckled.

"I don't know, but I did. Anyway, I pulled her name up on our data software and her records couldn't be accessed."

"So, let me guess. You want me to see what I can do about finding out what's in the file?" Peter questioned.

"Yeah. I need to know more about this girl, Peter."

Peter and I sat and talked a little longer before I had to leave to pick up Juliette. It was too late to call his friend at the bureau to find out about Juliette's sealed record. Given how young she looked, it couldn't be too bad. If I had to guess, maybe a few misdemeanors, and since she was considered a minor, that would explain the sealed record.

While I headed to the front door, Peter stayed behind to make sure everything was locked up at the shop. As I got into my truck, I felt the vibration of my phone in my pocket. Pulling it out, it was a text message.

Juliette: I have decided to take a cab home. No need for you to pick me up. See you at your house.

Me: No need to call a cab. Already en route to pick you up, be there in a few.

Juliette: Not sure when I will be off.

Me: Then I will wait until you are.

Juliette: DON'T!

When I got her last response, I knew something more was going on with her than having to work late. Starting my truck, I headed in the direction of the distribution center. I had a pretty good feeling that she wouldn't be there. As I was driving down Broadway, something caught my eye as I was stopped at a stoplight across the way. It looked to be a woman being forced into a Lincoln Town Car. When the light changed, I just missed hitting the car as it pulled out in front of me. I could barely see who was sitting in the back, but I would know that profile anywhere. *"Juliette, what the fuck?"* I was so confused by what I saw that the honking from behind didn't even faze me, until cars began driving around me.

Taking my foot off of the brake, I tried catching up to the Lincoln, but it was too late. I needed to improve my skills in following cars. Losing sight of a bus was one thing, but now this; it was unacceptable in my book. Knowing that I had missed out again, I took a deep breath of regret and turned down the next block in order to get to my place. The only thing I could do was to wait for Juliette to arrive home and question her then.

The house was dark when I pulled my truck into the garage. I didn't know what I was thinking. I was hoping that she was already here so we could have our little talk. Heading inside, I went to the fridge and pulled out a cold one. Popping off the cap, I took a long pull and walked over to the living room where I knew I wouldn't miss her coming home. The minute she walked through the door, she was going to have some explaining to do.

I wasn't sure how long I had been sitting on the couch before I dozed off. If it wasn't for the sun shining through the window, I might have still been sleeping. Pulling my cell from my pocket, I pressed the 'on' button to bring it to life. It was seven in the morning, way past the time that Juliette should have been home. Thinking that I might have missed hearing her come in, I got up to check. Knocking lightly on her bedroom door, there was no answer, I turned the knob and pushed open the door to find that she hadn't been home. Her bed was still made and her things were still on top of it. There was only one place I knew she could be. Grabbing my jacket, I headed out to her place. Since it was a beautiful morning, I decided to walk.

While I was on my morning walk to Juliette's house, I kept thinking about what I was going to say to her. I knew she didn't know me that well, and giving me an explanation for last night was probably not going to happen. The most I could ask for was that she trusted me enough to tell me if she was in some sort of trouble. The way that man forced her into the Town Car last night wasn't normal, and her resistance was proof of that.

Looking down the road, Juliette's house came into view. Just by looking at it, it appeared that no one at home. Knowing that her car was in the shop and wouldn't be ready until the end of the week, there was the possibility that she was home. When I reached her door, I knocked lightly and waited for her to answer. After about the third time, I was just about ready to give up and check the back door, but the door slowly opened. When she appeared, I couldn't believe what I saw.

CHAPTER SIX

Juliette

The look on Ash's face said it all the minute I opened the door. If I'd had a little bit more time, I would have been able to hide the bruising under my right eye. I knew I should have contacted Ash when I got home and let him know that I decided to tough it out at my place.   Watching the look on his face go from concern to anger, I finally said, "Don't look at me that way. It's not a big deal. I ran into the wall."

"That looks like more than running into a wall, Jules. It looks more like you ran into someone's fist." he replied with a serious tone.

"Well, it wasn't a fist, trust me," I countered confidently. Leaving him standing at the front door, I yelled over my shoulder, "Would you like some coffee?"

"Are you changing the subject? How is it that you can make coffee anyway? I mean, with there being no water." Ash questioned.

"I bought a jug of bottled water on my way home this morning. There are just some things a girl cannot go without, coffee being one of them," I replied.

As I began pouring Ash a cup of coffee, it dawned on me how horrible I must look. Not only did I have a black eye, I had a pretty good idea that my make-up was smudged, making my eye look worse than what it actually was. Handing Ash his cup, I tried to keep my head low, so that he couldn't get a better look at me.

Before I could take the first sip of my coffee, Ash asked, "So are you going to tell me why you insisted on not being picked up after work?"

Placing my cup on the counter, I turned my head away from him and gazed out the small window in the kitchen. I knew he was waiting for an answer by the way he was tapping the teaspoon on the counter. Without even thinking, I said bluntly, "Because I didn't need you to come after me. You probably have better things to do than being my chauffeur all the time."

"I told you that I didn't mind doing that for you. If I had something else that I needed to do, then I would have told you," he began. "There is one thing I don't understand."

"What's that?" I asked hesitantly.

"Why would you be getting into a Lincoln Town Car when you were supposed to be at work?" he asked sternly.

Shocked by his question, one thought ran through my mind. *How in the hell would he have known that?* I was very careful. He was nowhere near when I hopped the bus transit to the Mandarin, and for him to see me get in the car at the club couldn't be possible, unless he had been following me the entire time. If that was the case, how much did he actually know and how much did I need to share with him? My gut told me that the best thing to do was to play stupid.

"Why would I be getting in a Town Car? It must have been someone else," I responded, moving to the sink to place my half-full cup of coffee inside.

I tried to keep my distance from him, but when he came up behind me, there was something about him being so near. The heat of his body was pressed so close to mine that I

63

could feel it burning into me. I was so afraid to move for fear that he would suck me into a place that I couldn't be. When he placed his hands on my waist and turned me to face him, it was all over. Even with my eyes closed, trying to shut out what was about to happen, I knew I would never be able to stop the magnetic pull.

"Jules, look at me," I heard him command in a gentle voice.

Opening my eyes, they met his for just a moment before his lips met mine. The gentle touch had my head spinning. It was so much different than what I was used to. My mouth parted, willfully letting him in. The message of his kiss sent a current of desire through me that made my body began to shiver with delight. Never had a man kissed me before, so light and delicate, like the warmth of a summer breeze grazing my lips. It was something that I needed more of.

When Ash broke the kiss, my eyes slowly fluttered open. It was as though he captured every emotion possible and I just stood there unable to say or do anything. *How could a kiss from one man have such an effect on me?* My head finally stopped spinning and I slowly moved away from him. If I stood close to him any longer, I wasn't sure what would happen. Rounding the counter, I looked over to him for a brief moment before I asked, "Can we head on over to your place? My things are still over there and I could really use a shower."

"Sure," he answered, placing his hands in his pockets.

Without another word to each other, we headed out of my house and down the road to his house. It was a beautiful morning and the fogginess in my head was beginning to clear. As we walked side by side, I could feel the brush of Ash's hand against mine, until he finally took hold of it and brought my hand to his lips. It was the sexiest thing I had ever seen. Trying to show him that I was unaffected, I dropped my hand from his and stuck my hands in my pockets. Looking down the road, I needed to say something to rid the silence between us.

"So, after I finish my shower, do you think we could work on getting my water up and running?" I asked hesitantly.

"That's the plan. I think I have what we need to get it fixed in the garage without going to town. You take your shower, I will see what I can find," Ash said with a smile.

As I walked in the direction of the guest room, I remembered what happened last time. "Wait, I need a towel."

"Oh, yeah, right," he began. "Wouldn't want a repeat from yesterday, although I didn't mind."

Waiting for Ash to walk pass me, I followed him to the linen closet, which was located just across the way from the guest room. He could have just told me where they were. He handed me the soft towels and I went to the bedroom, while he headed to the garage to get what he needed to fix the plumbing in my house.

I hated the fact that I wasn't able to take a shower when I got home. I also hated the fact that I had the scent of that man on my body. I couldn't wait for the day when I would finally be done with this and be able to move on. Turning on the water in the shower, I went to the bedroom and gathered the things that I needed while the water warmed up. Setting my things on the counter, I slipped off my clothes and opened the shower door. The water felt so good on my skin.

Not only did I have a nasty black eye, my body felt like it had gone through hell, which technically it had. As I stood in the shower and let the hot water scorch my body, I thought about my life up to this point. I wasn't sure when it got to be so complicated. That was a lie, and I knew exactly when it became so complicated. It was the day that I thought I needed that Ruby Red Matte lipstick. It was the day that I met him. The man who would show me the difference between controlling my freedom and having my freedom controlled. That was five years ago. In exchange for my freedom, he promised that no one would know what happened that one miserable day, but mostly, my mom would never find out.

Rinsing the conditioner from my hair, I finished washing the remaining lather from my body and turned off the water. While still in the shower, I grabbed a towel and wrapped it around my soaked hair. I wrapped the other towel around my body and tucked the end between my girls to keep it in place. Even though I felt cleaner, I wasn't feeling any better about the job assignment last night. At least, that was what I preferred to call it.

As I looked in the mirror, I knew that I could make this life go away and have the life that I dreamed of since I was a young girl, but having that would mean telling my mom the truth. I would no longer be the best thing that ever happened in her life. I would be just another disappointment to her, and I wasn't willing to be put in the same category as my dad.

Pulling the towel from my hair, I tried to think of something else. I didn't want to ruin my day thinking about my pathetic life. Walking over to the bed, I opened up my bag, which was still on the bed, and searched inside for my cute pair of panties and the matching bra. Stripping off the towel, I started putting them on. When I was dressed, I headed back to the bathroom to see what I could do about covering up the shiner that I had under my right eye. I knew I shouldn't have argued with Sebastian. He owned me and I should have obeyed him no matter what the request, but with what the client wanted to do me, I just couldn't agree to it. But in the end, I ended up doing as he asked anyway.

Looking ten times better than I did earlier, I headed out of the bedroom and down the hall to find Ash. Thinking that he might be in the kitchen, I walked in that direction. He wasn't there. I remembered him saying that he thought he

68

might have the materials needed to fix the plumbing problem at my house. I walked over to the door leading to the garage and turned the knob. Just as I opened the door, I could hear the sound of music playing. He had to be there. He came into view as I walked down the steps. He was looking through a tub filled with various objects that looked to be related to things you would use for plumbing.

I didn't want to scare him, so I lowered the volume on the stereo. The minute he looked over to me, I waved my hand and said, "Hey."

Smiling at me, he asked, "How was your shower?"

"It was wonderful. Thank you," I replied. Stepping closer to him, I looked inside the tub to see if I could tell what he was searching for. "Are you finding what you need?"

"Yep. I think your plumbing will be fixed in no time," he said.

Putting the items that he didn't need back into the tub, he took hold of it and placed it back underneath his work bench. I watched as he put the pieces together like a puzzle.

He then grabbed a few other items and walked over to where I was standing. Looking at what he created, he held it up and said, "I think this will work to fix the leak."

Nodding my head as if I knew exactly what he was talking about, I turned and headed back up the steps leading to the kitchen. Before I opened the door, I said over my shoulder, "I'm going to grab my things. I'll be right back."

~****~

When we got back to my house, it was already late morning. I was hoping that Ash would be able to get what he needed to get done with the plumbing before it got too late. My body was exhausted and the only thing that I wanted to do was go to bed before I had to go back to work.

Walking to the front door with my keys in my hand, I noticed a package leaning up against the screen door. I was pretty sure that Ash spotted it as well. Picking it up, I put it underneath my arm and stuck the key in the lock. As I pushed the door open. I heard Ash's comment, "Secret admirer."

Looking over to him, I said, "Right," before I placed the package on the coffee table and headed to the kitchen. I knew that he would be following me there. Opening the fridge, I asked, "Can I fix you a sandwich or something before you start?"

"Nah, I'm good," he replied.

"Alrighty then," I said as I pulled out the bread, some lunch meat, lettuce, and the mayo.

While I was fixing myself a sandwich, Ash began working on the sink. Placing the knife in the mayo jar, I stopped mid-scoop as Ash slowly peeled off his t-shirt. I had never seen so many muscles on one guy in my life. It wasn't the only thing that got my attention. The tattoo that he had on his left shoulder was amazing. It looked like it could have been something tribal, like a flame or something. I couldn't help but stare at it. Men with tattoos weren't my thing, but in Ash's case, it suited him.

Moving my eyes from his Adonis body, I focused on making my sandwich. Just as I was ready to bite into it, Ash mumbled something from under the sink. Walking over to where his body was sprawled out, half inside the cupboard and half resting on the floor, I crouched down and asked, "Did you say something?"

"Yeah. Can you hand me that wrench?" he asked between grunts.

I had no idea what a wrench even looked like, but there were only two tools lying on the floor. One of them I knew was a screwdriver, so the other one had to be a wrench. Picking it up, I turned towards him and placed it in his hand that he had held out for me. Rising to my feet, I went back to the counter where I set my sandwich.

Taking a bite, I stood and watched him work. Not even a movie could beat the show I was currently watching. Whoever said you can't have your cake and eat it too didn't have one Ash… something-or-another in their kitchen. With every bite I took, his muscles flexed as he tightened the pipe under the sink. Even the muscles in his stomach were working overtime.

When I finished enjoying not only my sandwich, but the view as well, I walked over to him and asked, "How much longer until I have water?"

"It should be right about now," he answered as he scooted out from under the sink. "Let me turn on the main water line and we will give it a try."

Ash headed down the steep stairs to the basement where the main water switch was. I waited in the kitchen until he returned. When he came back, he took the faucet handles, one in each hand, and began turning them until the water began to run. At first there was a sputter and then a spatter until the water began flowing smoothly. Squatting down, Ash checked under the sink to make sure there were no leaks from his handiwork. Washing his hands under the stream of water, he said, "I think it is good. There aren't any leaks that I can see."

"Thank you for fixing that for me," I replied as I handed him a dish towel to dry his hands.

I wasn't sure what was going on between us, but when Ash took the towel from me, instead of drying off his hands, he took the ends and swung it over my head and wrapped it around my waist, pulling my body closer to his. I lost my balance and my hands ended up on his hard chest to steady myself. It was like I touched a magnet. The feel of him beneath my hands drew me in, leaving me completely breathless.

I was unable to look him in the eye. Ash let the towel drop to the floor as he moved his hands to cup my face. He lifted my head with a gentle touch and our eyes met. That was all it took, for at that moment, I was his. His mouth captured mine and the heat of his lips warmed my soul. The kiss sent a strange tingling sensation down my body that gripped me like a vise. My lips parted and he swept his tongue inside. It was like heaven the way he consumed me. Every touch was more tender than the first.

Without a warning, my body was up off the floor and wrapped tightly around his. I felt as though I couldn't get enough of him. He was strong, passionate, and sexy as hell, and for now, he was mine. Walking over to the counter, he gently placed my bottom on it while keeping his soft lips attached to mine. Taking my hands from around his neck, he lifted them above my head and slowly began pulling my tank top up over my head. With a gentle sweep of his hand down my arm, he looked down at me and whispered, "I can't resist you any longer."

Placing my hand under his chin, I lifted his head until his eyes met mine. With a breathy voice, I commanded, "Then don't."

Our mouths collided with each other, but this time there was a hunger between us that needed to be fed. While Ash was unclasping my bra, I was working to get his jeans undone. My efforts were stopped midstream the second Ash placed his mouth on my nipple, which sent a stream of pleasure to the very tip. He continued to kiss and suck my throbbing peak while his other hand gently outlined the pink tip of my other nipple. I lost all concentration on setting his shaft free. My mind was reeling with ecstasy at the attention he was giving my breasts. I lost all hope of taking control of the situation, which I was groomed to do so many times before, when his lips left my breast and the warmth of his breath took its place, sending a shiver through my body. It wasn't because if the coolness of his breath, it was because more than anything I wanted this man to take me.

With my mind clouded in pleasure, I managed to get his jeans unzipped; the feel of his arousal was evident through the material of his briefs as my hand followed the trail of hair that led to the present that waited for me. Pulling his shaft free, I caressed the tip with my thumb, feeling the drop of precum that had been resting on top. Gliding my hand down the length, I could feel his cock thicken as I tightened my grip as best I could around it.

My movements were stopped when Ash lifted my butt from the counter and pulled down my shorts and panties in one swoop. I knew I was clean, but like with every other man that had fucked me, I wasn't taking any chances. In a heated breath, I moaned, "Do you have a condom?"

With his mouth next to my ear, fondling the lobe between his teeth, he whispered, "Right front pocket."

Lowering my hand, I found the right pocket of his jeans and pulled out the condom. Since I didn't want him to stop what he was doing, I placed the end of the small package between my teeth and ripped it open. Pulling the latex sleeve free, I placed it on the tip of his impressive cock and carefully rolled it on. I wasn't sure if he was impressed by my handiwork, but his appreciation rang clear as he said, "Nice."

Pushing my knees to my chest, Ash slowly began moving inside me. Every inch that he pushed, my passage was stretched wider to accommodate his size. If I hadn't learned self-control all those years before, I would have let go the minute he thrust inside me. Never had anything felt so good as the sensation of him moving in and out of me. As he continued to sink deeper inside me, I could feel my self-control begin to fade. My walls began to tighten and the release I had been holding on to demanded to be set free. With a moan of euphoria, my body shuddered with delight.

Holding on to Ash like he was my saving grace, my emotions got the best of me as my tears began to fall. Wiping them away as quickly as I could, I released my hold on him and willed my mind to hide the emotions that this man had brought out. Feeling the sensation of his bliss, I waited a moment for his body to relax before I kissed him on the lips and said, "Shower time," as though what just happened had no effect on me.

CHAPTER SEVEN

Ash

When Juliette got up, there was something going on with her other than just needing to shower. She might have tried to hide it, but I knew what just happened between us had an effect on her. Watching her leave, I couldn't help but watch the way her body moved with every step. If I wasn't careful, the semi-hard erection I had would soon be a full-blown raging tower ready to explode.

Pulling up my boxers and my jeans, I walked over to the sink to get cooled off. Turning on the faucet, I splashed a handful of water on my face. Even though a shower would have been better, I did manage to tame down my arousal for the time being.

While I waited for Juliette to finish her shower, I decided to investigate where she got the package from. I wouldn't be able to open it, but at least I would know who it came from. When I picked it up, it almost felt like there wasn't anything inside. Looking at the sender's address, I pulled my cell from my back pocket and took a quick picture of the mailing label.

I opened the door and wandered out the front to see if there was anything else I could do for Juliette. One thing I did notice was that the siding below the front window was beginning to come loose. I walked over to my truck and grabbed my hammer from the back seat. When I turned to walk back to the house, I noticed a black sedan coming up the road. It seemed odd since the only place that it could be going was either here or to my place. Waiting for the sedan to come closer, I kept an eye on it as it passed Juliette's house and continued driving in the direction of my house.

Getting a good look at the driver, I could tell that there was only the chauffeur and someone seated in the back. I couldn't a good look at the passenger since the windows were darker than what was legal. I also missed getting the plate number since my focus was more on who was inside. My only option was to wait until they came back and get it then.

About fifteen minutes passed, the car still hadn't come back, which told me that they had to be at my place. Going back inside the house, I needed to let Juliette know that I had to take off for a few minutes. As I walked back to her room, I could no longer hear the water running in the shower. I tapped lightly on the bathroom door, thinking that she was probably getting dressed. With no response, I tapped again and asked, "Jules, are you in there?"

The room was silent. There was something going on, and as usual, I was thinking the worst. Turning the knob I opened the door and found that she wasn't inside. Leaving her room, I began checking the house to see if I could find her. She was nowhere to be found. I even checked the back of the house, knowing that she wasn't in the front. Still no Juliette. I had no idea where she could have gone, but I knew I needed to get to my place and find out who was in that car.

Climbing in my truck, I began driving up the road when I saw the sedan coming my way. I looked down to where the plate should have been, but there was nothing there. Looking in my review mirror as it passed, I looked below the trunk and found there was no plate there either. I found this to be rather odd, unless of course it was a new vehicle purchase, but even then, there should have been a paper plate on it. My next conclusion was that whoever was inside didn't want to be known. That would certainly explain the dark window.

Once I reached my house, I stopped the truck in the front without driving it into the garage like I normally did. I had no idea what was going on, but my first instinct was to check out my house. Taking out the revolver I had hidden away under the front seat, I checked to make sure it was loaded before heading up the steps to the house. Unlocking the door, I opened it slowly. I wasn't sure what would be waiting for me and I wasn't about to take any chances.

After spending about an hour searching the house, everything seemed to be in order. Nothing seemed to be disturbed, but that didn't mean that it wasn't. Thinking I would rather be safe than sorry, I decided to get in touch with Peter. I wanted my place swept from top to bottom. The last thing I needed was to have any surprises come at me that I couldn't see. We had the best equipment possible at the shop that could detect if there were any bugs or cameras placed in my home.

Peter assured me that he would be at my house in about an hour with a couple of the guys to search my house. After hanging up with him, there was only one other thing that I needed to take care of, and that was to find out what happened to Juliette. Dialing her number, I waited for her to answer. After just one ring, her phone went to voice mail, which told me that her phone had been turned off. I wasn't sure what was going on with her, but I had at least an hour to find out. Jumping in my truck, I headed back to her place to see if there was anything there that would tell me more about her. I was pretty sure that her house was still unlocked since I neglected to lock it before I left.

When I arrived at Juliette's, the house was pretty much the way I left it. My hammer was still sitting on the front porch, and the door was open with the screen door closed. Getting out of my truck, I grabbed my gun, which I'd set on the seat beside me, just in case there were any uninvited guests inside. Opening the screen door. I looked around and listen for any noise. I was pretty sure that it was only me in the house. Beginning my search, I noticed right away that the package Juliette had received was gone from the coffee table. I wasn't sure when it had been moved or taken as I didn't pay attention to it earlier.

I figured that the best place to start searching would be her bedroom, and the closet was typically the one place girls tended to put things they didn't want anyone to see. Sliding back the closet door, I began examining its contents. There were a lot of shoe boxes on the top shelf, which was an excellent place to keep things hidden. Pulling down the first box, I looked inside to find a pair of expensive looking heels. I recognized the signature red bottom and knew that they were Louboutin's.

A confused thought had crossed my mind, *"How does a simple girl working in a distribution center afford designer shoes?"* Placing the shoes back in the box, I pulled down another box with another pair of designer shoes. Box after box, every one carried the same thing. It just didn't make sense. Either Juliette had a rich boyfriend, or worse, was doing something other than working at a distribution center to make her money. Even going through her clothes showed designer labels, most of which were fancy-looking evening gowns and dresses.

Closing the closet, I began looking through her dresser drawers. This was another place that girls tended to hide things. There wasn't anything out of the ordinary in them: bras, panties, stockings, and other girly treasures. All of which were very sexy. Closing the last of her drawers, I went to the nightstand. Another place to hide things. Pulling on the top drawer, I found it to be locked.

I walked to the kitchen to see if I could find something to jimmy the drawer open. Grabbing a knife that I thought would work, I headed back to Juliette's room. It took some doing, but I was finally able to get the drawer open. Rummaging through the contents, I found some childhood trinkets, which weren't really anything special. A set of jacks and a ball, a couple of small figurines made of plastic, and a fake ring from a bubble gum machine. When I dug further in the drawer, I found an envelope stuffed way back between some other papers. Opening the envelope, I pulled the contents out. Unfolding papers, it appeared to be some sort of document.

I was only able to read the first line, which read, 'Contract of Ownership' before the screaming sound of a mad woman sounded behind me. "What the fuck do you think you're doing?"

I tried to explain, but all I got was a slap across the face before the papers I was holding were ripped from my grasp. Shocked, I just stood there speechless. I had never seen a woman angrier than Juliette. Trying to tone down her anger, I began to explain, "Jules, hold on. It's not what it looks like."

"Get the fuck out of my house, Ash. You had no right. Just leave," she ordered.

84

As I walked to the front door, I noticed that the package she had received was opened with the contents draped across the couch. It was a black gown with diamonds along the straps and front. Juliette could be angry all she wanted, but eventually I was going to find out what was going on with her. Hearing the screen door close behind me as I left, I looked up just in time to see the back end of the sedan I had seen earlier. Running after it, I thought that I might be able to get a glimpse of the person sitting in the back. Unfortunately, the only thing I was able to see was the back of a man's head and his jet black hair.

Getting in my truck, I drove back to my place. I knew that Peter would be there soon to sweep my house. Maybe he would have insight on what to do to fix my problem with Juliette. I knew that he and his now-wife Lilly had a lot of problems before they finally worked through it. It was time for a little male bonding. Maybe he would be able to give me some advice on how women worked.

When I got to my place, I pulled my truck in front of the garage. It wasn't long after I got inside that I heard the engine of Peter's Camaro pull up. Looking out the window, I could see that Sly, Lou, and Mike were also with him. I headed to the front door so I could help them unload the equipment that they were pulling from the trunk of Peter's car. Jogging down the steps, I walked up to the guys and said, "Hey, guys, I really appreciate you doing this for me."

"Not a problem, Bro," Lou said with a smile.

"Hey, who is your new neighbor?" Mike asked as he pulled a computer from the trunk.

"Her name is Juliette Daniels. She bought the place about a month ago. Peter, do you have a minute to talk?" I asked, looking over to Peter.

"Yeah, sure. You guys go ahead and get started. We'll be up in a few," Peter said.

Peter and I began walking to the back of the house where I knew we would be out of earshot from the guys. It wasn't that I had anything to hide. It was just that the guys always seemed to make a joke of things, especially when it came to women troubles. When we reached the back, I walked over to the fire pit and just looked down at the ashes that were still sitting on the bottom. Peter came up beside me and asked, "So what is this about, Ash?"

Gazing out to the wooded area a few yards from where we were standing, I tried to find the right words to ask for his advice. "Do you remember when you and Lilly first met and all the problems you two had to tackle?"

"Yeah, I remember. We were both stubborn, but our love for each other finally won out," Peter answered.

"Well, the girl I've been telling you about..." I began running my hand through my hair, more nervous than I had ever been. "I'm kind of falling for her, but I'm afraid that she is hiding something and it could change everything."

"Listen, Ash, I'm no expert when it comes to relationships, but I know that if you really care for this girl, whatever she is hiding will surface and you two will be able to work it out. I truly believe in chance meetings and things happening for a reason. Don't stress out. Just take it day by day."

I knew that Peter was right. Maybe I was making more of this than needed. But one thing I knew for sure. Juliette was beyond pissed when she caught me looking through her things. She had every right to be. I could kick myself in the ass for going through her things. Not because I got caught, but because I should have waited until we knew each other better and I earned her trust. Now I wasn't sure I would ever gain that.

After our little talk, Peter and I headed back to the house to check on the guys. As we were going in, Mike was coming out looking at something in his hand. Almost bumping into us, he said, "Holy shit. Sorry, guys."

"What do you have there, Chavez?" Peter asked.

"I found this under your lamp in the living room. It looks to be some sort of microphone. The other guys are still searching the rest of the house. I just wanted to show you what we found so far," Mike responded.

"This is too fucking much. Why the hell would anybody be bugging my house and how the hell did they do it so fast? This is so fucked," I said, getting more pissed by the minute.

"My guess is that they knew exactly what they were doing. Maybe we can trace where this device was purchased. There should be some sort of serial number on it. We'll get to the bottom of this, Ash," Peter assured me.

"I hope you're right, Bro. I hope you're right."

CHAPTER EIGHT

Juliette

I wasn't sure if I was angry with Ash or surprised to find him in my room going through my things. Holding the contract in my hands, my blood began to boil. I hated that I was forced into signing the stupid contract to begin with. I should have just taken my chances, spent my time in juvie, and been done with it.

Looking down at the letter, I began reading the contents. *This is a binding Contact of Ownership between Sebastian Collins (Master) and Juliette Daniels (Slave). The so forth mentioned Slave shall at all times seek the Master's comfort, pleasure, and happiness, above all other considerations the Slave may have. The Slave agrees that she shall abstain from her own pleasures and will only be allowed to be pleasured by her Master. The Slave also agrees that she will at all times and places submit to her Master's wishes no matter what that entails. Per failure to do so, the Master has the right to terminate this contract or handle any disobedience on the Slave's part however he sees fit. The*

Slave will work to keep her body, mind, skills, and attitude in an acceptable condition that will please the Master's desires. The Slave also understands and agrees that if she doesn't meet these requirements to the Master's satisfaction, it will be sufficient cause to administer any punishment that the Master deems necessary. The Slave will accept her punishment with no resistance, no matter how painful, uncomfortable, or unpleasant it may be for her. Furthermore, this contract can never be broken except by the Master, and only in the event of said Master's death or the sale of said Slave for ownership. Being of sound mind and without influence, Juliette Daniels agrees to enter this contract under her own free will. Signed this 27th day of March.

I couldn't stand to read any more of this stupid contract. Crumpling it up, I threw it back in the nightstand drawer and locked it away. As I sat on the bed, I brushed my fingers along my black eye and was reminded of what happened the last time I voiced my opinion. I knew this had to stop. This was no life and I couldn't continue living like this. Pushing from the bed, I pulled out my cell and called for a ride.

When the taxi honked, letting me know that it had arrived, I checked my appearance one last time before I left to meet it. I knew I couldn't go the way I was dressed if I was going to get inside the Collins office building, so I decided to change into a light blue sheath dress and a pair of cream colored sling-backs.

As I rode in silence to Manhattan, I kept thinking about what I was going to say to Sebastian. I knew that whatever it was, it had to be convincing, and I had to show him that I wasn't afraid, nor was I going to put up with his shit anymore.

When the cab driver pulled up to the Collins Building, I scooted my body over and looked up at the tall building, remembering the day that I was first taken here. Paying the driver, I opened the door and walked toward the entrance. Taking a deep breath, I opened the heavy glass door, pulled my shoulders back, and walked in with confidence. Today was either going to be a very good day or the worst day of my life.

Entering the elevator, I watched as the floors began increasing on the LED panel. Before long, the doors opened and I met my destiny. There, standing next to the reception desk was Sebastian Collins, the man who was no longer going to have control over me.

As he looked over to me, I could see the shock on his face as he grinned, his mouth thinning with displeasure. "Juliette, this is a surprise."

"This is going to be more than a surprise once I tell you what I have to say," I responded, staring into his expressionless eyes.

Looking over at the young girl, who looked more like a pinup model for Playboy, he said, "Hold all my calls, Sasha."

Her named fit her perfectly. *"Sasha, the big-boobed bimbo, want-to-be porn star,"* I thought to myself as I followed Sebastian down the long hallway to his office. I knew this walk all too well. I might have been afraid as an eighteen-year-old, but no more. I had grown up a lot in the past five years and this man was no longer going to intimidate me. Stepping into his office, it still looked the same and smelled of his scent as it did five years ago. Taking his place behind his enormous desk, I waited just inside his office door, a relatively safe distance from him.

Placing his hands on his desk, he commanded in an icy tone, "Don't stand there looking like an insecure child, have a seat and tell me what this visit is about."

There was always something about his voice that sent chills up my spine. Not moving an inch from where I was standing, I looked at him with confidence and said abruptly, "No, what I have to say won't take long."

"I don't like where this is going, Juliette. Say what you have to say."

"I want out of the contract. I am no longer going to let you control my life," I began, feeling the tightness in my chest intensify. "I'm going to turn myself in. I should have done this a long time ago. I am no longer going to be your slave. Ever!"

It felt good to stand up to him. Turning to leave his office, I heard the pound of his fist against his desk. "Stop," he demanded, his voice cold and exact.

I couldn't turn to acknowledge his demand. I stood still and said the one thing that would end this for good. "I'm done."

"Are you so sure, Juliette? You better think twice about what you are saying. By the way, how is your new friend? I believe his name Ash. Yes, Ash Jacobs."

Unable to control the fury that was ready to burst inside me, I turned to Sebastian and asked coldly. "The guy at the hardware store, was that your doing? Leave Ash out of it. He has nothing to do with this."

"Are you so sure? I would certainly hate for anything to happen to him because of your disobedience. Stop this foolishness. I expect you to be ready by 9:00 this evening," Sebastian ordered as he sat back down. Before I had a chance to argue, he continued. "Don't be late, Juliette. You know how I hate tardiness."

Leaving his office, I couldn't even think straight. The one thing I didn't count on, he dangled in front of me. There was no way I was ever going to get out of this contract. I would be his prisoner forever. He would never let me go. Getting outside the building as fast as I could, the only thing that I wanted to do was drink until I was completely numb. Standing on the sidewalk, I looked across the street and spotted a small restaurant with tables sitting out front. Crossing the street, I went inside and looked around for the bar. The minute I saw it, I headed over to the bartender, who was pouring a round of shots of something amber in color.

Taking a seat, I said, "I'll have one of those."

The bartender pulled out another shot glass and filled it to the brim, then placed it in front of me and said, "That will be seven dollars."

Reaching in my purse, I pulled out a ten and laid it on the counter. The liquid burned as it ran down my throat. Unable to speak, I gestured to the bartender to pour me another. Shot after shot, my body was beginning to feel numb. I wasn't sure how many shots I actually had. I lost count after number three. I was just ready to ask for another when the bartender came over and said, "Sorry, Miss, but six is the limit. How about a tall glass of water?"

I was in no mood for water, so I stood, ready to leave to find a different place that was willing to serve me. I felt numb, but not numb enough for what was waiting for me at nine o'clock. Pushing from my barstool, I said, "I'm good, thanks," before I gave him a five dollar tip and left.

I think the bartender might have been right about the six drink limit. Sitting down and drinking was a lot different than standing and trying to walk. I may have had a little bit more than I should have. Stumbling out of the restaurant, I opened the door and was hit by the sunlight, another thing I wasn't prepared for. I wasn't sure if it was the brightness or the six shots, but all I could feel was my body getting clammy before I lost my balance and fell to the sidewalk. Feeling dizzy and unable to breath, the liquor took over, and my world went black.

~****~

My eyes slowly fluttered open as I began to feel the aftermath of the alcohol I consumed. I could no longer feel the hardness of the concrete beneath me. The surface under me was soft and plush. Pushing to my elbows, I tried to clear my head before I took in my surroundings. Regaining my clarity, I could see that I was somewhere unfamiliar to me. Looking around the room, it looked to be a hotel. A very expensive one, at that, based on the furnishings and the fact that there was a sitting area and an en suite. Pushing the covers off of my body, I was only wearing my bra and panties. This was not a good thing. Not only because I was half naked, but also because I couldn't remember how I got that way.

Swinging my legs over to the side of the bed, I stood, trying to gain my balance. My head hurt like hell, but no matter how much it hurt, I was more concerned about getting out of this place. As I was standing and feeling a little wobbly, I heard a knock on the door. Looking down at my body, there was no way I was going to answer the door in this state. Hurrying to the bathroom, I searched for a robe, which I found, nicely folded, on the marble vanity. Slipping it on as quickly as I could, I went to the door.

Standing on the other side was a hotel waiter with a cart. As I glanced down to the cart, I saw several dishes covered with stainless steel globes, a glass of orange juice, and a carafe of what I presumed was coffee. Before I could question who had ordered the food, the waiter said, "Mr. Collins thought that you might be hungry."

Stepping aside, I allowed the waiter to come in and watched as he rolled the cart near the sitting area, where there was a small table and two chairs by French doors that led to the balcony. When the waiter was finished setting the dishes on the small table, I looked at him and said, a little embarrassed, "I'm sorry, I don't have any money to tip you."

"Not a problem, Miss," he began with a smile. "Mr. Collins has taken care of it. Enjoy your breakfast."

Knowing that it was the afternoon when I left the bar, I turned to the waiter and asked, "Can you tell me what day it is?"

Staring back at me with a confused look, he replied, "Why, it is Tuesday, Miss."

I lost three frickin' days. I couldn't believe that was even possible. The only good thing that came out of my stupidity was that it was no longer Saturday and I didn't have to face the man who would be my assignment for the night. Out of all my assignments, he was the one man that I always dreaded being with. Sebastian knew how much I loathed this man and the things he did to me. He never seemed to care. As long as I came back to him in one piece, it was all business to him.

I will never forget the first time Sebastian introduced me to Mr. Marlow. He should have been called something else, like Mr. Stench. It really didn't matter since all my assignments were addressed as either Sir or Master. Mr. Marlow was as ruthless as he was round. He always smelled of cigars and mothballs. That wasn't even the worst part about him. It was the things he did to me. Just like clockwork, whenever I had to go with him, he always ordered me to kneel before him and kiss his feet. It was so degrading. Then, once the greeting was done, he would pull me to my feet by my hair and force his sandpaper lips to mine.

Sitting down at the small table, I had no appetite, so I poured a cup of coffee and continued thinking about what my fate was going to be. Anything would be better than spending time with Mr. Marlow. I suddenly lost my desire to have coffee as soon as the memory of our last encounter entered my mind. The place he had taken me was no better than a place a pig would bunker down. I remember the horrible smell of sweat and urine. I was so afraid that I would end up dying in that room. It was only when he reminded me of my responsibility to him that I pushed what was about to take place away and thought about a beach and the heat of the sunshine warming my body. It was the worst thing I had ever been through. His body was pressed so close to mine that I could almost taste the cigar smell that lingered on his tongue when he kissed me. It was as though I had smoked it myself. But I knew when he bent his head and kissed me, I had to control my disgust for this man. His hands would always wander down my body, stopping at my breast. The way he touched me was like a vise. When he took hold of them, he gripped them so hard, like they were nothing more than a fruit than needed to be squeezed in order to get the last drop of juice from them.

When he tore my blouse completely off, I was ready to put an end to this torture. If it hadn't been for his threat, I would have left. But this man had no morals and his control over the situation gave me no other option but to submit to his callous treatment of me. Stripped completely from the waist up, I would never forget the feeling of his mouth on my nipple. Never had a man done to me what he did. Not only did he coat it with his slimy saliva, he bit it to the point of almost breaking the skin. Someone needed to give him one-on-one instruction on how to properly handle a woman's breast.

Lost in thought, I barely heard the knocking at the door. Pushing from the small table, I went to the door to answer it. The minute I opened the door, I tried to close it on the man standing on the other side. My efforts were useless.

He managed to get his foot in the door and weasel his way inside the room.

"You've been a bad girl, Juliette," he said in a nasty tone.

"And you disgust me," I remarked.

I should have thought first before I let my feelings for this man get the best of me. No sooner than the words left my lips, his hands were wrapped around my body, holding me painfully close to his. Having a hangover and smelling the scent of his breath so close to me was not a good mix. I could feel my stomach begin to churn and I didn't realize he had brought two guests with him.

"Take hold of her. I think it is time that this little wench be taught a lesson on how to show respect," he said with a hint of sarcasm.

When the two men took hold of me, I knew I had lost my chance to escape. Their hold on me was too tight. Walking me over to the bed, one of the men let go of me while the other tightened his grip on me. My back was towards the door where Mr. Marlow was standing, but I knew the minute he walked up to me. Smelling his cigar filled breath next to my ear, he ordered, "Strip her completely,"

I did the only thing I could think of. I pleaded, "Please, Mr. Marlow, don't do this. I'll do whatever you ask."

CHAPTER NINE

Ash

I was really beginning to get worried. I hadn't seen or heard from Juliette for three days. Every day I had gone by her place, trying to apologize for what I had done, but she wasn't there. I even went as far as purchasing her a bouquet of flowers, hoping that she would forgive me. Even though I didn't know her that well, I knew this wasn't like her. Something happened to her the day we got into a fight. My only other choice was to go back to her place and do some more investigating. Though I knew there could be a chance that she would show up, I had a good feeling that she wouldn't.

Grabbing my jacket, I headed to her house. Even though there was a chill in the air, it was still nice enough to take a walk. The best scenario would be for her to be there safe and sound. With the moon guiding me to her house, I began thinking of all the things I wanted to say to her once I got there.

Finally reaching Juliette's, all the lights were off, which told me one of two things. Either she was home and safely tucked in bed, or she still wasn't home. Hoping I was wrong about her not being home, I knocked on the door. Looking over to the where the doorbell was, I made a mental note to fix it the next time I came over. With no answer on the other side, I decided to take a chance and go inside. Pulling my handy lock-pick kit from the pocket of my jacket, I took two pick tools that I always used and began working the lock. Hearing a click, I pushed the door open.

Playing it safe, I used the light of the moon to guide me through the house until I could get to the kitchen, where I knew there was a flashlight. Grabbing the small flashlight from the kitchen drawer, I turned it on and proceeded to the bedroom, where the one item that would tell me what was going on with her would be. Sitting on her bed, I began picking the lock to her nightstand. Once I had it open, I pointed the light towards the drawer and began searching for the envelope that held all the answers. It wasn't hard finding it since it was at the front, empty. Reaching toward the back of the drawer with my hand, I found a crumpled up wad, which I knew was what I was looking for. Straightening it out, I began reading what it said.

At first, I couldn't comprehend what I was reading, then it began making sense. The fancy clothes, the secrets, and the Lincoln Town Car. The more I read, the more I thought, *"What kind of trouble is she in?"* I knew that this type of thing was out there, but for it to be so close to home, that was just unheard of. Placing the contract on the bed, I separated the pages and took a picture of them with my phone camera. This was way above my head, but maybe Peter would have some insight on this kind of thing.

It was getting late, and I had searched every inch of Juliette's house. I didn't find anything else that would tell me more about her. Making sure that everything was put back the way I found it, I left her house, locking the door behind me. On the walk home, I couldn't get that contract between her and Sebastian Collins out of my head. First thing in the morning, I would be heading to the shop to see what I could find out about him. My guess was that he was the same man that I saw in the Lincoln a few days ago and the same man that had my house bugged.

~****~

The next morning when I woke up, I took a quick shower, grabbed a cup of coffee, and headed out. I didn't want to waste any time getting to the shop. Driving by Juliette's house, I decided to check one more time to see if she was home before I headed into the city. With my truck still running, I opened the door and walked over to the house. I pulled open the screen door and knocked on the door. I knew that it was a waste of time since I was just here less than five hours ago, but at least I tried.

When I got to the shop, there was no one there. It was a perfect time to do some checking. Unlocking the door, I headed to the conference room and booted up the laptop that was sitting on the table. While I waited for it to come alive, I decided to make a pot of coffee. I knew that Peter and the guys would be coming in soon and would appreciate having coffee already made before they started their day.

Pouring a cup, I headed back to the conference room and began my search regarding one Mr. Collins. There wasn't very much about the man on the Internet except that he was deemed one of the most ruthless businessmen in New York and he had his hands into everything. He had an office building in Manhattan, which was known as the Collins Building.

Thinking that there had to be more to this man than his business practices, I decided to call the one man who would know more about him, being a businessman himself. Pushing from the long table, I headed to Peter's office to see if I could find the number of Rade Matheson in his Rolodex. We had done some work for him in the past and occasionally he still used Jagged Edge Security for his annual charity events.

Flipping through the cards, I finally found his number. Taking my cell from my back pocket, I dialed his number, hoping that it wasn't too early for him.

"Matheson," he greeted me.

"Rade, hi. It's Ash Jacobs with Jagged Edge Security," I answered.

"What can I do for you, Ash?" he asked in a serious voice.

"Have you ever heard of a man named Sebastian Collins?"

"I've had my share of dealings with the man. If you ask me, he is an arrogant bastard who likes to play by his own rules," Rade offered.

"What else do you know about him? Do you think he would be the kind of man that would hurt anyone?" I asked.

"What is this about, Ash? I get the funny feeling that this might be more personal than just a friendly inquiry."

"You could say that. I found this contract between him and a friend. After reading it, it sounded like he pretty much owned her soul. I'm talking about Master and Slave shit."

"Sebastian Collins isn't a man you want to mess with. He has been known to have a dark side. I would steer clear of him," Rade suggested with a hint of concern in his tone.

"I'm not so sure I can do that, but I will keep your suggestion in mind. Thanks for the information, Rade."

"Ash, one more thing."

"What's that?"

"Be extremely careful and watch your back," he remarked.

"Always am. Thanks, Rade."

Ending the call, I began thinking about what Rade said. Even though Rade had a dark side, I knew he was a good man. I also knew he was serious when he said to be careful. I had a funny feeling that Mr. Collins was a man that didn't like to lose. I'd stake my life that he was the reason behind Juliette's black eye.

Walking to the kitchen to grab another cup of coffee, I heard the front door to the shop open. Peeking around the corner, I could see that it was Peter. Just the man I needed to talk to. Watching him head to his office, I grabbed another cup of coffee for him and made it the way he liked. Light and sweet. By the time I finished and got to Peter's office, he was already sitting behind his desk getting ready for the day. Setting his coffee in front of him, I took a seat in one of the chairs in front of his desk.

"You're here early," he commented, grabbing his coffee and taking a cautious sip.

"Yeah, I had something that I needed to do," I replied.

"Well, you'll be glad to know that my friend was able to get information on the sealed records for Juliette Daniels. Looks like she got into a bit of trouble when she was eighteen. Theft mostly, but it looks like there was a charge for trespassing and breaking and entering. She never did any time for it."

"Does it say anything about why her records were sealed?"

"My guess is, because of her age and the offense. Anyway, that's all there is," Peter indicated.

"Thanks for the info. Any news on the new mission?"

"Should hear something today. Be ready."

"You know me. Always on standby," I answered with a chuckle.

Rising to my feet, I said good-bye to Peter and headed to my truck. One thing I knew for sure, I needed to check out the Collins Building and have a little chat with Mr. Collins. Since Juliette wasn't around to give me answers, maybe he could. Starting the engine, I looked in the review mirror to see Cop and Sly pulling in. I gave them a quick wave as I continued backing out.

As I got closer to the city, I was glad that I lived in a small town. The traffic was unbearable as I turned on Madison Street and made my way to Seventh Avenue. Looking at the address that I had written down, I checked the huge buildings for the address until I spotted the one that had S. Collins Building in blue steel lettering on the front. While I drove down the street trying to find a place to park, a car pulled away from the curb. I pulled into the spot before anyone else had a chance to take it. Feeding the meter, I headed to the entrance.

Not only was the traffic unbearable, but the number of pedestrians on the sidewalk was unbelievable. It was almost like fighting off a crowd of spectators at a crime scene. Fighting my way through the foot traffic, I finally reached the building and opened the door. I will never get used to the hustle and bustle of a big city. It seemed as though people were always in such a big hurry.

Looking at the directory, I found that Mr. Collins' office was located on the top floor. *"Go figure,"* I thought to myself. There were thirty-five floors to this building. As the elevator door opened, I just stood there. My body began to tense and I could feel the rapid beat of my heart. I knew I had two choices, either get on the elevator and ride it to the thirty-fifth floor or take the stairs. Unwilling to take my chances with the elevator, I chose to take the stairs. Finding the exit sign, I walked over to the door, opened it, and looked up as far as I could. Taking a deep breath, I began making my way up the stairs.

Halfway up, I stopped a moment to take a breather. I was in the best shape I had ever been in, but climbing those stairs was definitely a workout. Catching my breath, I began climbing the remaining stairs. When I finally reached the top, I had to take another breather. Looking down at my watch, it had taken thirty minutes to make my way to Sebastian Collins' floor; it was thirty minutes I didn't have.

Opening the door, I was greeted by a blonde that looked like she just stepped off the set of a triple-X movie.

113

Stepping up to her desk, I couldn't help but notice the silicone breasts that were staring at me like they were ready to burst out of her blouse. Keeping my eyes focused on the wall behind her, I shot out, "I'm here to see Sebastian Collins."

"Name?" she asked, dragging out the word.

"Ash Jacobs," I answered.

While she let the bastard know that I was here to see him, I took in my surroundings. It looked pretty impressive, but not as much as he would like to think. The paintings on the walls seemed to be originals and the quality of his furnishings appeared to be top of the line. Even though it screamed success and power, it didn't impress me.

Taking a seat on the plush leather couch, I took the most recent copy of *Gentleman's Quarterly* from the small table and began skimming through the pages. I really wasn't a fashion kind of guy, but it was either that or *Better Housekeeping*. Throwing the magazine on the small table, I ran my hands through my hair, a little annoyed that I had been kept waiting. Standing to my feet, I was just about to check with 'Bambi' to find out what was going on when a medium build man with jet black hair wearing a black pinstriped suit came walking down the hall. If I had to guess, it was Sebastian Collins.

With his hand held out, he asked in an arrogant tone, "You must me Ash Jacobs?"

I gave him a strong grip and said, "And you must be the ruthless businessman Sebastian Collins."

I don't think he appreciated my sarcastic tone by the way he gave me a disgusted look as his jaw clenched and his eyes became a darker shade of brown. "No need for the harsh words, Mr. Jacobs."

Sidestepping from me, he raised his hand outward, signaling for me to proceed ahead of him. Walking down the hall, I heard his deep voice behind me. "Last door on the right."

Taking his instruction, I entered the office on the right. When I felt I was far enough inside the room and he was standing before me, I bluntly asked, "What is your relationship with Juliette Daniels?"

Looking up at me with a raised brow, he said, "She is an employee of mine. Although, I'm not sure that is any business of yours."

"It is my business. Where have you taken her?" I hissed, stepping closer to him, getting a better look at his features.

Sebastian walked away from me and towards a cart on the far end of the room which held a couple of decanters containing liquor and four matching crystal tumblers. Without looking at me, he asked in an icy tone, "Drink?"

"No," I snapped. "The only thing I want is answers. What did you do to her?"

"Now, now, Mr. Jacobs. Don't let your imagination get the best of you. Miss Daniels is on an assignment. She is currently out of town and won't be back for a couple more days. I'm sure she will tell you all about it once she returns."

CHAPTER TEN

Juliette

I had no idea that my little visit with Sebastian would cause me such pain. I also needed to remember that three shots of whiskey were my ultimate limit. Lying on the king-sized bed, feeling like my body had just been crucified, which technically it was, I thought about what he did to me and why I wasn't strong enough to stop it. More than Sebastian, I hated Mr. Marlow. His definition of domination was inflicting as much pain as possible on a woman's body. What I hated the most was that Sebastian knew exactly what kind of man he was and allowed him to do whatever he wanted to me.

Pushing from the bed, I went to the bathroom for a much needed soak. The minute I saw myself in the mirror, the tears began to fall. I didn't even recognize my own body. I endured the blunt torture he put me through, but I had no clue that my body would look as though I had been used as a pin cushion. My nipples were a fire red with dark red bite marks circling the outer edge. There were also bruises

117

trailing down the valley between my breasts all the way to my pelvic bone. As I touched the tip of my nipple with my finger, I noticed the dark rope burns around my wrist. Feeling humiliated, I dropped my gaze to the tile floor, only to notice the same burn marks around each ankle.

I could no longer hold on to my strength. My body gave way and I fell to the floor as the memory of what happened sunk in. The tears spilled, with no desire to hold them back. I screamed with anger, knowing that everyone on the hotel floor could hear me. It was the only way I could escape the feeling of shame and outrage building inside me. All I wanted was to remove the dirt from my body. Turning the water on in the tub, I got it as hot as I could.

When I stepped inside the enormous tub, I felt nothing. Not even the heat of the water burning my skin fazed me. No matter how hard I scrubbed, I couldn't get rid of his scent. My skin began turning raw. With the heat of the water and the rubbing, it felt like my skin was on fire. I finally calmed and leaned my head back against the rim of the tub. Hearing only my breathing, I sunk lower in the water, until my head fell below the waterline. The only thing I wanted to do was close my eyes forever and never feel the way I did.

~****~

Beep..., beep..., beep... I heard somewhere in the distance. At first I thought I might have been dreaming. Slowly opening my eyes, I realized that it wasn't a dream at all. I was no longer in the hotel suite, but in a room that smelled like antiseptic. As my eyes began to focus, I knew I was in the hospital. The beeping sound got louder, and I looked to my right to see a heart monitor and some other monitor beside me. Pushing up to my elbows, I noticed that my body was no longer hurting.

Just as I was about to get out of bed, a nurse entered my room. "No, no, Miss," she warned. "You need to stay in bed."

She walked over to the side of the bed and helped cover me up again. Checking the IV drip to make sure it was still flowing properly, she looked over to me and asked, "Do you think you are up to talking to the police? They've been here for some time waiting to speak to you."

"I'm not sure why they would want to talk to me," I replied.

119

"Well, just like with all cases, the hospital has the authority to contact the police if they feel that a patient has been abused, and in your case they did."

Everything came back to me. The ropes, the whip, Mr. Marlow and his men. There was no way I would ever be able to tell the police what happened. Even though the evidence of abuse was all over my body, I had to figure out an explanation.

When the nurse left and the two officers walked in, my head cleared and my story began coming together. Pushing to a sitting position, I looked at the officers and confessed, "You are wasting your time. Aside from waking up in the hospital, I can't remember anything."

One of the officers pulled out a notepad and began thumbing through his notes. Clearing his voice, he said, "It appears that you were spotted on Madison Avenue leaving Cello's pub and Grill."

"By whom?" I hissed, curious to know how they would know that.

Flipping through the pages, he licked his thumb as he turned each page. Stopping, he replied, "Mr. Collins. He was the one who called 911. He pulled you from the tub. He thought maybe you might have fallen asleep, or worse, tried to commit suicide. He also thought that your wounds may have been self-inflicted."

I could have screamed. It was true that I wanted my life to end, but self-inflicted? They must have been crazy. The worst part of this whole thing was that I couldn't say anything about what really happened.

"I don't remember any of that, but if Mr. Collins said that was what happened, then it must be so." The best thing for me was to play dumb.

"We will find out exactly what happened. A woman police officer will be in shortly to do a thorough examination with one of the nurses."

"And if I refuse?" I questioned.

"I guess our other option would be to have a full psychiatric evaluation done," the officer replied, giving me a smug look.

121

I knew I wasn't getting out of this. They would soon know what actually happened to me. There was no way I was going to be put in a nuthouse. It would be so much worse than the life I had now. The only thing I could do was to pray that Sebastian wouldn't punish me for what I had no control over. Rolling over to my side, I turned away from the officers. Both of them left the room full of themselves.

A short time later, a nurse showed up with the woman police officer wanting to poke and prod at me to find out the real truth. Drawing the curtain, the officer introduced herself as Officer Hanes before she began cleaning under my fingernails. As the officer was doing her thing, the nurse began laying out some items on the small tray, which I assumed was some sort of rape kit. My breath hitched, which caused both of the women to look at me with concern.

"Don't worry. It is no different than getting a Pap smear, Miss Daniels. It is a little uncomfortable, but otherwise pretty painless," the officer said.

Having a swab shoved inside my vagina wasn't the problem, it was what they would find that had me concerned. I was pretty sure that even though I saw Mr. Marlow sheath his stubby little cock, he pulled it off before he entered me.

122

The only thing I could hope for was that the bath I took washed all the remnants of the assault away.

The nurse took another swab and shoved that one up my ass. I knew they wouldn't find anything. As sadistic as Mr. Marlow was, anal sex wasn't his thing. I was thankful when the rape examination was finally over. The only thing left to do was to take pictures of my body. Standing to my feet, I untied the strap behind my back and pulled the gown off my body. Nothing had changed since the last time I looked at my body except the additional welts where I tried to scrub off the grime. After turning me this way and that way, they were finally done with their examination.

When the nurse pulled open the curtain, my chest began to tighten. Ash was standing on the other side, leaning up against the door frame. He was the last person that I wanted or needed to see. His eyes met mine and I knew then that concern was in them. Nodding to the woman officer and the nurse as he let them pass, he walked over to the bed. His eyes were no longer making contact with mine. Instead, he was looking at my chest where my gown had accidentally fallen when I got into bed. Pulling it back over my shoulder, I reached behind my back and began trying to tie it, with no luck. Ash must have sensed my frustration, because he was soon beside me.

"Let me help you with that, Jules," he said in a soft, comforting voice.

When the strap was secure behind my neck, he stood beside me with that same look of concern on his face. Unable to stand it any longer, I place my hand on his and said, "It isn't as bad as it looks."

"What the hell happened to you? I've been at your place every day for almost a week. I even went to your boss's office trying to find out where you were."

"You did what?" I questioned, making sure I heard him correctly.

"I went to see Sebastian Collins, your boss. He said that you were out of town on assignment. By the looks of it, it looks like you went to a lynching instead of an assignment. What is going on, Jules?" he asked, his body becoming tense, giving him a couple of inches in height.

"I was out of town on assignment."

124

"Do you mind telling me how you happened to get all banged up?"

"I don't remember." Just like with the police officers, I was going to stick to that story.

"I don't believe that for one second," Ash snarled, raking his hands through his hair and turning his body away from me toward the window. "I read the contract, Jules. I know all about your Boss, or should I say Master? Is that what the tattoo is about? Some sort of mark of ownership?"

"How could you know that? Unless you went inside my home again, without my permission. How could you?"

"It wasn't like that, Jules. I knew how angry you were. When I went back to apologize for what I did, you were gone. For four days I went to your house and you weren't there. I got worried," he began, walking back over to the bed where I was boiling with anger. "I really care about you, Jules. I thought that if I took a look around your house, I could find out what happened to you."

"So, you went back to seek out that damn contract, just like you did the first time?"

125

Everything inside me burned like a volcano wanting to erupt. He had no right snooping inside my home. I knew the minute he saw the contract the first time, I should have put that damn thing somewhere else. It still was no excuse for what he did.

"Yeah... I mean, no... I just wanted to know who you are. I don't care about that stupid contract. The only thing I care about is you and what happened to you," Ash paused before taking my hand in his. "Jules, what happened to you? Where were you?"

"It doesn't concern you, Ash. How can I ever trust you again?"

I knew my words hit him like a big tank. I couldn't trust him. Even though we had a moment together, it wasn't an open door to allow him to dig into my personal life. It was my choice if I wanted to share my past with him. He had no right to that contract.

"It does concern me, Jules. Everything about you concerns me. Did Sebastian Collins do this to you?" he questioned, pulling his hand from mine and waving it in a circular motion over my body.

126

I don't know what got into me, but everything suddenly let loose: the anger, the tears, the pain. "I can't do this anymore."

I wasn't sure where my strength came from, but the IV was out of my arm and the stand holding the bag fell to the floor with a loud crash. Before I could get out of bed, Ash had his arms around me, holding me as tight as he could. I tried getting away from him, but his hold on me was too strong. My body finally relaxed and the rush of adrenaline that surfaced moments ago was gone, leaving me exhausted and drained. The only thing that felt good was the warmth of Ash's body as he pulled me closer to him.

Even speaking in a hushed voice, I could hear the vibration in his throat as he said, "Shhh... it's okay, baby. Everything will be okay."

Looking at him with tear-drenched eyes, I uttered softly, "That's just it, Ash. It won't. It will never be okay."

CHAPTER ELEVEN

Ash

When the nurse came in to reinsert Juliette's IV, it was the perfect time for me to re-evaluate the situation. Walking down the hall, I spotted the police officers that had questioned Juliette. One of them was Officer Caleb Stevens. I knew him very well from assistance calls that were initiated by Jagged Edge Security. Taking a chance that he would remember me, I walked over to the two men and called out his name as though we were best buds. "Caleb, hey, do you have a minute to talk?"

Looking over to me, I could tell he knew me. Holding out his hand, he said, "Ash, from Jagged Edge. How the heck are you? It's been a while."

"Yeah, it has. I guess one would say that is a good thing," I replied.

"So, what can I do for you?"

Walking away from his partner, Caleb followed my lead. When I was sure I was out of earshot, I asked in a lower than normal tone, "You and your partner questioned Juliette Daniels. I wanted to know if you had any information on what happened to her."

"I don't mind sharing what we found out. You guys at Jagged Edge are top notch. You have certainly made our jobs easier," he began as he patted me firmly on the shoulder.

"I appreciate the compliment. We know how tough it is out there. That's one of the reasons Peter started the company in the first place. Anyway, about that information."

"So, it seems that Miss Daniels doesn't remember anything that happened to her, which I personally think is a crock of shit. I think she knows exactly what happened to her and she is protecting someone else or herself. Her boss, Sebastian Collins, is the one who made the call."

"How much do you know about Sebastian Collins, Caleb?" I asked, trying to plant a seed in his head so that he would dig into him.

"He isn't a person of interest here, so not a whole lot. Do you think he had something to do with this?"

"Damn straight. When did he make the call?" I asked, planting another seed.

Flipping through his handy notebook that he pulled from his back pocket, he found what he was looking for and said, "It was early this morning, around 1:00 a.m."

As Caleb moved the pages back, his eyes began to focus on something else. "What is it, Caleb?" I asked, knowing his little mind was spinning with information that he was putting together.

"It's just that... Umm... Miss Daniels was seen at Cello's... wait a minute, that was five days ago. It doesn't make sense. Unless..." Caleb said, scratching his head.

"Unless what, Caleb?" I asked

"Okay, here is the thing. Mr. Collins admitted seeing Miss Daniels at Cello's and she appeared to have been intoxicated, according to him. Given her state, if I were a gentleman, I would have made sure she got home okay. So,

130

the question here is, what was she doing at the Four Seasons, and why was her boss there with her five days after the initial encounter at Cello's?"

"I would say that you just made Sebastian Collins a person of interest. Thanks for the info, Caleb."

As I walked away from Caleb, I couldn't help but turn my head back towards him. He was a funny guy. The way he began piecing things together reminded me of the reruns of "Columbo" that my grandfather use to watch. At least now there was a reason to start looking into Sebastian Collins, and with the contract he had with Juliette, I was pretty confident that something would eventually surface without my input.

The nurse was just leaving as I entered Juliette's room. She seemed a lot more relaxed than she did twenty minutes ago. If I had to guess, the nurse probably gave her something to calm her down. Pulling up a chair, I took my place beside her bed. The green of her eyes were like glass as she looked over to me. There was something about the way she looked at me that suggested she wanted to say something. Just when I thought she might, her eyes shut and remained that way as one last deep intake of air sounded before she fell asleep.

~****~

I wasn't sure what possessed me to sleep in the hospital chair next to Juliette's bed all night long when I could have spent it in the comfort of my own bed. Stretching my achy body, I headed to the elevator to get some much needed coffee from the cafeteria before Juliette woke up. When the doors opened, I could believe who was on the inside. He was the last person I expected to see.

"What the hell are you doing here?" I growled as he shifted the bouquet of roses he was holding in the other hand.

"I was just about to ask you the same thing," he said between gritted teeth.

"Juliette is in no condition to see visitors, at least not you."

"Well, I'm pretty sure you don't have the authority to stop me from seeing my star employee. Now if you will excuse me…"

Before I could lay into him, one of the nurses on duty came up to us and warned, "Need I remind you gentlemen that this is a hospital and not Madison Square Garden? If you have a problem, take it outside."

The nurse was right. This was neither the place nor the time to get into a fight with this man. Letting him pass, I got onto the elevator as he got off. As the door closed the last thing I could see was his smartass grin as he looked over his shoulder. I might have let this go this time, but soon enough he would get his.

By the time I had returned to Juliette's room with my coffee, Sebastian Collins was already gone. The expression on Juliette's face said it all. Something had happened during his visit. It wasn't only her expression that was a dead giveaway. The roses that he had brought her were not in her room like I would have expected, but sitting on the counter at the nurses' station in a glass vase.

Concerned, I took a seat beside her bed and asked, "That bad, huh?"

"I wish he would have never showed up," Juliette confessed.

"Yeah, he looked pretty full of himself when I met him in the elevator," I admitted, looking into her worried eyes. "Whatever is going on, Juliette, would you please let me help you?"

"I'm beyond help, Ash. Even if you could help, you don't know what Sebastian is capable of."

"How about you let me worry about that?"

Just when I thought Juliette was about to open up to me, the nurse stepped in, letting us know that the doctor had released her from the hospital and that she could go home. The timing couldn't have been any worse. Even though Juliette was relieved to be leaving, I wasn't so sure that she would tell me anything once she left. The moment of truth was gone.

While the nurse was getting Juliette ready for her release, I went down to the parking garage to get my truck so I would be ready for her when she made it to the lobby. Getting in my truck, I noticed a note of some kind under my wiper. Standing on the running board, I reached over the windshield and grabbed the note. As I unfolded the paper, there in black ink it read 'STAY AWAY FROM JULIETTE.' Knowing the precautions that I should have taken beforehand, I placed my index finger and my thumb in the corner of the paper and held it lightly as I searched the glove box for something to put in. I always kept a few plastic bags in there just in case the time would come that I needed one. Placing the note in the bag, I laid it in the glove box and started the engine.

Juliette was already in the lobby waiting for me when I arrived. Climbing out of the truck, I rounded the front so I could assist her. Once she was safely inside, I reached over her and locked the seatbelt in place. As we pulled away, there was only one thing on my mind and that was her safety. In a stern but caring voice, I said, "You're staying at my place. I don't want you to be alone. It's not safe."

Just when she was about to argue, I looked over to her with my signature 'Don't bother' look before she could say a word. I heard a hitch in her breath and knew she understood the look loud and clear.

There was silence the whole time we were in the truck. It was only when we neared her house that she said, "We need to stop at my house so I can get a few things."

Nodding my head, I pulled up in front of her house. I wanted to get this over as quickly as possible and get her inside my house where I knew she would be safe. When Peter and the guys found the cameras and bugs in my home, Peter suggested I get a surveillance camera of my own. Taking his advice, I installed five cameras in all, two in the back and three in the front. I hooked them up so that I could monitor any activity on my laptop computer. The equipment was state of the art and cost me a pretty penny. If it worked, it would be money well spent.

It was a miracle how quickly Juliette gathered the things she needed and stuffed them into a suitcase. I had never seen anyone pack so fast. Loading up her suitcase, I put in the back seat and helped her in. Pulling away from the house, a thought had crossed my mind which brought a smile to my face. I hadn't realized that Juliette was looking at me until she asked, "What are you smiling about?"

"Just glad you didn't argue with me on this," I replied, knowing that wasn't the real reason for my smile.

136

Sure, I was glad that she didn't argue, but I also was thinking about all the fun we were going to have.

CHAPTER TWELVE

Juliette

The minute I saw a package stuffed between my front door and my screen, I knew exactly who it came from. After everything that had happened, I thought that Sebastian would have given me a break. I was glad that I told Ash I would only be a minute and there was no reason for him to come inside. Kicking the package inside was the only way I could assure that he wouldn't see it.

I made sure that the package was out of view before I grabbed it and took it with me to the bedroom. Tearing into it, I saw that it wasn't the typical gown that he always sent, but a black corset with matching panties and black stockings. Thinking that there had to be more to this outfit, I shook the box, only to have a white envelope fall to the floor. Looking behind me to make sure I was still alone, I ripped it open and read the contents.

'Be ready at 10:30 p.m. A car will be there to pick you up.

DON'T BE LATE!!!!'

I crumpled the note in my palm and threw it against the wall. There was no way, I would ever be able to meet Sebastian's car at 10:30. Trying to figure out what to do, I began shoving whatever I could find in my suitcase. It was the quickest I had packed in a long time. Looking down at the torn box, I grabbed the contents and stuffed them inside my suitcase as well as I could before I zipped it shut.

Ash had a look of amazement on his face as I opened the door. It was most likely due the fact that I was in and out in less than fifteen minutes. As he pulled away from the house, I couldn't help but think about the note. I knew that if I defied Sebastian and simply refused to show up, he would get his revenge on me and that revenge would be Ash. I couldn't let that happen. Somehow, I had to figure out a way to get back over here without Ash knowing or coming after me.

Ash took my suitcase from the back seat as I headed up the stairs. Looking over my shoulder to make sure he was behind me, I said, "I think I am going to take a quick shower and get some of this hospital stink off me."

Before I could open the door, he took my hand and pulled me closer. His mouth melted into mine as his tongue glided between my parted lips. The kiss ended much too quickly as he whispered softly, "I'll fix you something good to eat." Looking up to him, I nodded as he smiled and brushed a strand of hair from my face. "There should be towels in your bathroom."

Pulling away from his embrace, I walked up the remaining steps and opened the door to the kitchen. Grabbing the handle of my suitcase, I rolled it down the hall and into the room that would be my haven for who knew how long.

Things hadn't changed when I got to my room. Everything was still as perfect as the first time I set foot inside. The only difference was that there were actually towels waiting for me in the bathroom. Stripping off the scrubs that were given to me at the hospital, I turned the water on in the shower and waited for the water to get hot. While I waited, I looked at myself in the mirror and studied the bruises on my body, remembering each and every one of them. The rage began building inside of me. All I wanted was to break the mirror and shatter it to pieces. Looking around the room, I grabbed the small soap dispenser sitting on the counter and threw it at the mirror. It didn't do anything but bounce off of the hard surface. Screaming, I picked it up from the floor and threw it again. Over and over I threw it, wanting so badly for the glass to break. Suddenly, without warning, Ash's arms wrapped around me and held me close.

The tears fell uncontrollably, but more than that, my body needed to release the anger. Spinning around, I captured his lips with mine, kissing him with the force of ten women. I felt his hands glide down my back before he took hold of my ass and swooped me off the floor. The feel of his warmth radiating through his clothes to my bare skin wasn't enough. I needed to feel more. In an animalistic rage, I pulled and tugged on his shirt, frustrated that I couldn't get it off. It was only after Ash released my bottom and finished the job by tearing the thin material of his t-shirt in two that I finally got what I desired. He was gorgeous. I trailed my fingers over the tribal tattoo on his shoulder before I placed my lips on it. With rushed kisses, I trailed them up his neck to his throat, until I pressed them gently against his lips. His lips parted, allowing me to probe the warmth of his mouth as his tongue dipped inside mine.

Ash moved with me out of the bathroom and placed me gently on the bed. Standing before me in only his jeans, he leaned over me, placing his hands on either side of my body. Dipping his head, he kissed me lightly on the lips and said, "I want you so bad, Jules, but not like this."

"I need you, Ash, please," I pleaded.

He must have felt the strength of my need, because he pushed from the bed and began removing his clothes. Every muscle in his body began to contract as he once again leaned over me and kissed me on the lips. Ash slowly moved his body so that he was straddling me at the waist. My body was all his. He began placing light, warm kisses down my neck to the tip of my nipple, where he nipped and sucked it gently. With a soft swish of his tongue, he traced my hard bud in circular movements before engulfing it completely. While his mouth was doing its magic on my nipple, his hand was caressing the other, shattering the anger and rage from moments ago.

My head was spinning with pleasure. It was a pleasure unlike anything I had felt before. I began to feel a tingling in the pit of my stomach. All I wanted to do was drink in his touch. Wrapping my arms around his narrow waist, I pulled him in closer. Ash positioned his body between my legs and began lowering himself on me, just enough for me to feel the hardness of his cock brush against my thigh. His hand slid across my belly to my smooth mound. Kissing me gently on the lips, his mouth was soon making a path down my ribs to my stomach before it rested on my clit. I knew that he would find me wet and ready for him. With a moan of satisfaction, he spoke breathlessly, "Undeniably delicious. I am going to devour every drop of your sweet honey."

When his tongue dipped in my channel, my body began to quiver with uncontrollable joy, sending my body to a place it had never been before. Slowly the rush of ecstasy weakened as I savored the feeling of warmth taking over my body. Ash lifted his head and made his way up my body. The minute our eyes met, I could see deep inside them. There was something different about them. Comforting and passionate. When his hand came to my face, my heart was swept up by them as he said, "You are the most precious thing in my life. I'm never going to let you go."

"Ash," I breathed, unable to say anything else.

"It's okay, Jules, I know."

Did he really know? I had no idea, but he made me feel like I meant something, and when he entered me, his slow, gentle movements proved to me that his words were sincere. There was no urgency. Just sweet, heartrending tenderness as he pushed deeper and deeper inside me. When he reclaimed my lips, my emotions took over and the tears I tried so hard to hold back came tumbling down. I knew at that moment that he felt my pain. His movements increased and my walls tightened around him, bleeding him of everything he had been holding back. With his eyes upon mine, Ash rocked inside me in slow rhythmic movements as my body unleashed, taking all the pain and sorrow with it.

~****~

I wasn't sure how much time had passed, but the room was dark and I knew that it was nighttime. Looking to my side, Ash was sleeping soundly next to me. Carefully getting out of bed, I grabbed my cell and headed to the bathroom. When I brought up the screen, it showed that it was nearly 10:00 p.m. I only had thirty minutes to get back to my house before Sebastian's car would be waiting for me. Gathering the items I needed, I quietly tiptoed out of the room and down the hall to the guest bathroom.

144

Taking a quick shower, I dried off and put on the black corset along with the matching panties and stockings. I put my hair up and put on some make-up. There wasn't anything that I could do about the bruises that weren't covered by the skimpy outfit I was left to wear. Looking around the bathroom, there was something missing. My shoes. "Shit," I cursed, in a low voice. The last thing I wanted to do was go back into the bedroom where Ash was and risk waking him. It wasn't that far to walk with no shoes, so I decided to nix them and head out.

As soon as I opened the front door, a cool breeze hit my almost naked body. There was no way I was going to make it to my house without freezing my ass off. Opening the closet door next to the front door, I grabbed one of Ash's coats and slipped it on. I quietly shut the door and headed down the wooden steps.

The minute my feet hit the dirt road, I began having second thoughts about walking the mile to my house with no shoes on. It wasn't the smoothest surface to walk on and tiny pebbles were going to have a toll on my sensitive feet. Taking in a deep breath, I sucked it up and walked as quickly as possible, not thinking about the torture I was putting my feet through. I was thankful that at least there was enough light from the moon to steer me away from the bigger rocks.

With fifteen minutes to spare, I reached my house. The first thing I did was soak my feet for a few minutes to see if I could ease some of the soreness. No sooner than I got my feet in the tub of water, I heard the sound of a horn honking. I knew that I had only been soaking for a couple of minutes. Drying them off, I slipped on my black Pradas and headed to the front door. Sebastian didn't say anything about wearing a coat, so I grabbed my light trench coat to cover my nearly naked body.

Opening the front door, I was greeted with bright headlights shining right on me. They were so bright that I couldn't see anything. I only heard the voice that I had come to know so well. "Get in. Now!"

I wasn't sure what Sebastian's problem was. He was early and by no means was I late. Hurrying as fast as I could in my five-inch heels, I walked quickly to the car. He grabbed my arm with such force that I nearly fell on my ass. "What's your problem?" I asked as he shoved me inside the car.

"I don't have time for your nonsense, Juliette," he said as he got in the Town Car.

I was totally speechless. I had no idea what he was talking about and I wasn't about to entertain his grouchy mood. The driver backed away from the house and headed down the road. I wasn't sure where we were headed and I was almost afraid to ask. Taking a chance, I asked in a soft voice, "Where are we going?"

"To clean up your mess," he stated.

"What mess?" I questioned.

"It would be better if you learned how obey my requests instead of questioning my intent. Sit back and don't say another word."

I wasn't sure what game he was playing, but I went ahead and did as he asked and sat back and tried to relax. When his hand grabbed mine and he brought it to his lips, I thought whatever was going to take place wasn't going to be so bad, at least until he said, "I'm going to miss you."

A feeling of uneasiness washed over me as I tried to understand his words. Pulling my hand from his, I asked defensively, "What are you talking about, Sebastian?" When he didn't respond to my question, I asked again nearly yelling my words. "Sebastian, what are you talking about?"

"You should have done as you were told, Juliette. Now you will have to pay for your disobedience," he answered sternly.

I still had no idea what he was talking about, and somehow knew that I wasn't going to get the answer that I needed. Whatever he thought I did or didn't do, he was wrong, and I couldn't even argue with him about it because I had no idea what the flippin' hell he was talking about. Taking a deep breath, I sat back against the leather seat and tried not to worry about what was to come.

CHAPTER THIRTEEN

Ash

I had never slept so well in my life. Reaching across the bed, I felt an empty space that shouldn't have been there. Opening my eyes to make sure she wasn't just out of arms' reach, I looked over to where Juliette was supposed to be lying. Her side of the bed was cold, which told me that she had been out of bed for quite some time. Sliding out of bed, I grabbed my jeans and struggled to put them on as I began walking to the door.

I had hoped that she was in the kitchen preparing coffee or something. I was greatly disappointed when I saw there was no sign of her. Matter of fact, she wasn't anywhere inside the house. Opening the front door, I looked outside, but she wasn't there either.

Finishing getting dressed, I jumped in my truck and headed down the road to her house. Once I got there, it was quiet and looked as though no one had been here. I didn't even bother to get out. The only thing that crossed my mind was Sebastian Collins. Pulling my cell from my pocket, I took the chance that she would answer my call. Her ringback tone played *"All of Me"* before it went to voice mail. Throwing my phone on the passenger seat, I turned right and headed to the shop.

Even though it was still early, most of the guys were already there. Lou and Sly were in the small kitchen stirring up something to eat, while Cop, Mike, Ryan, and Josh were taking inventory at the direction of Nikki. She was one tough girl with everything she had gone through. It was hard to believe that she was now part of the team. She was still going through training, but she would definitely be an asset to the group.

After I greeted everyone, I headed back to Peter's office. He was the best person to get advice from without sugar coating it. Knocking on the door, Peter was on his cell and signaled for me to have a seat. Based on the conversation he was having, I was able to figure out that he was talking to Hawk. Hawk was a great guy and was an asset to Jagged Edge Security. I didn't blame him for leaving the security company to be with Isabelle in Kierabali. If I had been in his position, I would have done the same thing. The love for a woman is a lot stronger than anyone might think.

150

Peter ended his call with Hawk and placed his cell on his desk. Before I could say anything, he said, "Hawk and Isabelle are going to be coming back to the States for a while. He didn't want to miss Cop's wedding and he has volunteered to help us with the mission."

"That's great. It will be good to see him and catch up," I replied, before I said what was really on my mind. "I need your advice, Peter."

"Let me guess, Juliette," he contended.

"Yeah. Something is off about this whole thing. It just doesn't make sense. Sebastian Collins has some kind of hold on her. Why the hell would she even agree to that contract?" I vented. "Another thing, when I woke up this morning, she was gone."

Remembering the note that was left on my truck, I pulled it from my pocket and passed it over to him. "What is this?" Peter questioned.

"I found in under my wiper," I answered, scratching my head.

151

Looking at the note through the plastic, he was able to read what it said. "I'll have it sent over and have it checked for prints. My guess is there aren't going to be any, except yours. In the meantime, let me see what I can find out about Mr. Sebastian and his business dealings."

Leaving the shop, I decided to head back to Juliette's. I knew that there was a slim possibility that I would find anything, but I had to at least check.

~****~

The house was quiet when I entered. I had no idea what I expected to find. Walking past the kitchen, I headed down the hall and began opening the doors. When I got to Juliette's room, the only thing that showed any sign that she had ever been there were clothes lying on the floor and a package that was on her bed. Walking to the bed while still scanning the room, I picked up the box and looked inside it. It didn't surprise me that it was empty. Throwing it on the bed, I noticed a wadded piece of paper on the floor. Bending down, I picked it up and unfolded it. I wasn't too happy with what I read, but at least I knew exactly what happened to her. Looking down at my watch, it was just past nine o'clock.

Based on the note, nearly eleven hours had passed since she was supposed to meet Sebastian's car. Running to my truck, I opened the passenger door and grabbed my cell. "He has her, Peter. Juliette is with that motherfucker."

"Calm down, Ash. Where are you at?" Peter asked.

"I'm at her house."

"Don't leave, I'll be right there."

After I hung up with Peter, the only thing I could think about was Juliette. I knew that Sebastian was somehow responsible for putting Juliette in the hospital. She was in danger and I needed to find where she was. I could no more wait for Peter than I could let something bad happen to her. Getting in my truck, I backed away from her house and headed to Manhattan. There were two places that I needed to check out. I knew that time wasn't on my side.

Pulling up to the Four Seasons, I waved the valet away and said, "Leave it, I won't be long."

The way he looked at me, I knew he was about to say something, It was then that I pulled out my security badge, making him retract his thoughts. Going through the front entrance, I walked up to the registration desk and waited for an available employee. Standing there for five minutes was long enough. Showing my badge once again, I was able to get to the front of the waiting guests. Walking up to the next available clerk, I once again showed my badge and asked with authority, "Can you please let me know what room Sebastian Collins is staying in?"

It took her a minute to look at the badge. She was a lot smarter than the valet. "I'm sorry, sir, but I can't give you that information," she stated, annoyed by my arrogance.

"Look, Ms..." I paused as I looked at her name tag, "Harper. Either you tell me what I need to know or I will call the NYPD down here to assist me. I don't think you want the drama, especially here."

"My boss would have my ass if he found out I gave you this information, but having the NYPD here would be much worse," she confessed as she began searching the guest record on her computer.

As I waited for her to bring up the information, I looked around the hotel lobby. I had never been to the Four

Seasons and now I knew why. It was much too rich for my taste with its dark marble floors and high ceilings. The large round stained glass window high above the entrance was also over the top. Turning back to the check-in clerk, I watched her expression lift with confusion.

"Is there a problem?" I asked objectively.

"No, not really. Just a little odd. Mr. Collins has his usual penthouse suite, but he also has another room reserved. The accommodations are for a Mr. Walter Marlow," she responded.

"Just give me the room numbers?"

Having the information I needed, I decided to check out the first room, which was located on the 40th floor. There was no way in hell that I was going to climb forty flights of stairs. As much as I hated getting into an elevator, I decided to take my chances. Standing in front of the elevator, I waited for the doors to open. Waiting until everyone exited, I stepped onto the car and faced the back wall. I pushed the 40th floor and moved to the back of the car. Closing my eyes and taking deep breaths, I tried to calm my heartbeat as I felt the elevator began to move. There were only a few other people in the elevator with me and I could only imagine what they might have been thinking.

I heard the ding of the car as the doors began to open. It was the 40th floor. I had never been more relieved to find that the elevator was extremely fast in reaching the floor I needed to exit on. Looking over to the floor directory, I headed down the long hallway to my right towards the hotel room. This must have been my lucky day. A hotel maid's cart was parked just outside another room a few doors down from the room I needed to enter. Spotting the master key card on her cart, I hurried and grabbed it while she was in another room changing the sheets on the bed. Opening the door, I propped a trash can that I took from the bathroom to hold the door open long enough so I could return the key to the cart.

As I scanned the room, it looked like no one had been here. There were no personal effects that I could see and the room was made up like it was ready for a new guest. Opening the closet, I hit pay dirt. There was a suitcase on a valet stand, which was open to reveal its contents. I was shocked by what I saw. Pulling one of the items from the case, I had no idea what it was. It was a black ball that had two leather straps on each side. Based on the other items in the suitcase, if I had to guess, it had to be some sort of gag device.

All of the items were toys used for kinky sex play. I was no angel, but some of the items were way too kinky for me. Putting the gag ball back, I closed the door to the closet and continued searching the room. Walking inside the bathroom, there were various items that only a woman would use. I saw an expensive bottle of bath beads, a pink shaver, and various lotions and cosmetics on the marble vanity. Also on the counter was a hairbrush and a women's barrette. Picking up the brush, I looked at the bristles to find that there were several stands of red hair on them. This wasn't a coincidence. They had to be Juliette's. I had seen enough. Whoever this Walter Marlow was, he was a sick fucker.

Cracking the door open, I looked down the hall where the maid's cart was to make sure she was still doing her thing. Seeing that the coast was clear, I headed past her cart and to the stairs. The penthouse suite was on the 52nd floor and going up twelve flights of stairs was no problem for me.

Stopping in my tracks, I realized I would be needing a way to get inside the penthouse. Backing up a few steps, I grabbed the master key card from the cart and quickly walked down the hallway before the maid found out that her card was missing.

Taking the stairs two at a time, I found that I wasn't able to access the penthouse from the stairs. I had to take the elevator. As I got onto the elevator, I swiped the master card so I could gain access to the 52nd floor. No matter how many times I swiped the card, it would not give me the access I needed. The only way I was going to get inside that penthouse was with the help of Peter.

CHAPTER FOURTEEN

Juliette

When we pulled up to the Four Seasons, I knew that this wasn't going to be good. The last time I was here things didn't go so well. Sebastian exited the car and held out his hand to me. Taking hold of it, I slipped out of the seat, careful not to expose what I was wearing underneath. Going through the revolving door, we headed up the steps to where the elevators were. As we got onto the car, instead of pushing the 40th floor, Sebastian slid his key card in the slot and pushed the button for the 52nd floor. In a way I was relieved that he wasn't taking me back to the room that held so many bad memories.

When the elevator stopped and the doors opened, I couldn't believe how beautiful it was. The light marble floors were polished to a brilliant shine. What had me in awe was the four foot chandelier that hung high above the dining table. Pulling me from my thoughts, I heard him ask, "Can I get you something to drink?"

Turning his way, I replied, "Yeah, water will be fine."

"You're going to want something a lot stronger with what I have to tell you," he confessed.

"What's going on, Sebastian?" I asked as he passed me a crystal glass with an amber liquid, which I assumed was Scotch.

Before he could answer my question there was a ding from the elevator, letting me know that someone had just arrived. Turning in the direction of the elevator, my jaw dropped with disgust as the blood in my body began to boil. Looking at Sebastian, I hissed, "What the hell is he doing here?"

"Settle down, Juliette. Mr. Marlow has made a very generous offer that I simply couldn't refuse," Sebastian admitted.

"What kind of offer?" I asked, angrier than I was a few seconds ago.

"Meet your new Master, my pet."

"Are you kidding me? Do you realize what you have just done?" I screamed, my fist clinched so tight I could feel my nails digging into my palm.

"I do. It's just business, Juliette, nothing more," Sebastian answered, stepping closer to me and placing his hands across my arms.

"Don't touch me," I cursed. "Do you want to know why I was in that tub submerged under water? It was because of him."

Without any other option, I untied my corset and pulled it down my body to reveal what damage this man had done. Sebastian's eyes went dark with anger. Stepping away from me, he commanded in an icy tone, "Turn around, Juliette."

I turned around, only to be greeted by a smile attesting to his satisfaction for his handiwork. I could have screamed, but instead, I did what I should have done months ago. I caught sight of a letter opener that was sitting on the table between us and went for it. Sebastian must have sensed what I was about to do, because no sooner than I got to the table and grabbed the opener, his arms were wrapped around my waist holding me back. "Let me go, Sebastian. I would rather die than be with that man."

"Walter, I hope you have an explanation for this," Sebastian questioned.

"I had nothing to do with this. Your girl needs to learn how to tell the truth. I think the only way to deal with Miss Daniels' disobedience is with punishment. What do you think?" he asked, his eyes filled with a darkness I had never seen before.

"Sebastian, he is lying. You have to believe me," I pleaded, looking straight at Mr. Marlow.

"This is no longer my concern, Juliette. Mr. Marlow can do whatever he sees fit."

I couldn't believe that Sebastian would take his side and let their arrangement go through. I didn't know who I hated most, Sebastian for feeding me to this cannibal or Mr. Marlow for lying about what he did to me. It really didn't matter. I was never going to win.

Mr. Marlow walked up to me and grabbed me by the arm. "Pick up your things, Slave, we're going," he ordered as he looked to Sebastian. "Check your account, Collins, your funds should be there."

I pulled my arm from his grasp only to have my actions responded to with a slap across the face. Falling to the floor, I felt the gentle touch of Sebastian's hand on my arm as he helped me stand.

"Maybe this wasn't such a good idea, Walter," I heard him say.

"The money has been already deposited. A deal is a deal," Mr. Marlow hissed.

As we got onto the elevator, I could see the regret in Sebastian's eyes. Drifting my eyes to the marble floor of the elevator, the tears began to fall. I wished I had never left Ash. I wished I never opened that package, but most of all, I wished I had never signed that stupid contract.

~****~

Nothing could have been worse than the punishment that was in store for me when we got to the room on the 40th floor. The first thing that Mr. Marlow commanded was that I strip completely and kneel before him. I knew that if I didn't comply, my punishment would be ten times worse. Taking off my coat, I stripped off my panties and kicked off my heels before sliding the silky stockings down my legs.

Kneeling before him, I almost lost it as his tobacco-stained smile looked down on me. All I wanted was to get this over and done with. With a snap of his voice he cursed, "Aren't you forgetting something?"

"No, Master," I said as I leaned over and kissed his shoes.

"That's better. Now, to your feet, Slave," he ordered harshly.

I quickly got to my feet, only to be dragged by my neck to the bed, where he threw me upon it. I closed my eyes and prayed that this time he wasn't going to do to me what he did the last time we were together.

I could hear him backing away from me and opening the door to the closet. I knew exactly what he was going for. It was his bag of tricks. Holding my breath, I waited to see what he would be returning with.

"On your hand and knees, Slave," he ordered behind me.

Doing as I was told, I pushed to my knees and placed my hands, palm down, on the bed. I could smell his scent as he got closer. I was about to gag, but was stopped the minute he ordered, "Open your mouth."

Once again, I followed his instruction and opened my mouth. With my mouth opened as wide as it would go, he placed the gag ball between my teeth and secured it tightly at the back of my head. He knew how much I hated this. I think he got off on making me as uncomfortable as possible. There was a sudden snap and I knew that not only did he grab the gag ball, he also grabbed the long thin whip. This was going to be my punishment.

"I think fifteen lashes are in order. Don't you agree, Slave?"

I knew if I disagreed, he would only add more. So with a nod of my head, I said in a muffled voice, "Yes."

"Yes, what, Slave?" he snarled.

"Yes, Master," I replied, squeezing my eyes together to keep the tears from falling.

The first lash was hard and burned beyond belief. I continued to squeeze my eyes tighter as a tear escaped. Unable to hold back any longer, my eyes popped open as the twelfth, thirteenth, fourteenth, and finally the fifteenth strike hit my back. My body fell to the bed. The way my back felt, I knew that it looked like a road map.

Walking to the side of the bed, Mr. Marlow roughly removed the gag. The minute it was off, I looked at him and screamed as loud as I could. "I hate you, motherfucker."

With the back of his hand, he struck my face to show he was the master and I the slave. "I'm going to let that slide, wench. Get yourself cleaned up." These were the last words he said before he left the room. As much as I wanted to leave at that very minute, I knew that he would be standing on the other side of the door just waiting for me to make another mistake.

Lifting myself from the bed, I went into the bathroom and turned the water on in the shower. I couldn't even look at myself in the mirror. I was a pathetic, weak woman who couldn't even face the truth.

The shower did nothing to make me feel better. All I wanted to do was curl up into a ball and forget everything. Drying myself off, I grabbed the hotel bathrobe that was folded neatly on the marble vanity. I carefully put it on without causing too much pain to my back. Once I succeeded in doing that, I went back to the bed, pulled down the covers, and closed my eyes. The only thing that allowed me to sleep was the thought of Ash lying next to me, holding me tightly and protecting me from everything. As the thought of him seeped in, my eyes closed and my dreams began.

~****~

As we pulled away from the hotel, I could have sworn I had seen Ash pull up to the curb and get out. He had found me, only it was too late. I wished I could let him know where I was, but I knew the minute I did, Mr. Marlow would make certain that he would be taken away from me. The last thing he wanted was any distractions on my part. He wanted my full attention, and if it meant getting rid of anything or anyone who got in the way, he wouldn't think twice.

We had been driving for a while when the driver finally turned down a long driveway. I had never been here before. The drive was lined with trees that could have used some TLC. When we approached the mansion, I really began to worry. It was like something you would see in a horror movie. It reminded me of the house from the movie *Dark Shadows,* only in much worse condition. It looked as though it was just about ready to crumble to the ground. The brick was white with ivy making its way up the side. Even that was half dead. The roof was supposed to be covered with shake shingles, but most of them were missing. The circular drive was also missing some of the cobblestones, which explained the bumpy drive.

The driver got out of the car and opened the door, Mr. Marlow stepped out and held out his hand to me. As much as I hated placing my hand in his with his tobacco-stained fingers, the last thing I wanted was to get punished again. Sliding my hand in his, I felt a strong tug, which yanked me out of the car.

"This is your new home, my slave. What do you think? Nice, right?" he asked, admiring his dump of a house.

"Very nice, Master," I answered, keeping what I really thought of the place under my breath.

"I knew you would like it. Wait until you see your room," he said with a twisted grin.

Smiling at him the best I could, I began following him up the concrete steps to the front door. The driver who was in front of us opened the door and stepped aside so that we could pass. When I entered the mansion, the smell just about knocked me off of my feet. I couldn't help but cough as the musty stench entered my nose. "*God, please let Ash find me,*" I thought to myself, holding back the tears that were building inside me.

CHAPTER FIFTEEN

Ash

Peter reamed my ass left and right as I tried to explain why I didn't wait for him. With the information I shared, he started to settle down and listen to what I had to say. I was glad that I was only talking to him on my cell. If I had been in front of him, it might have been much worse. After hanging up with him, I told him I would meet him at the shop. We needed to do some research on this Walter Marlow and find out what his relationship with Sebastian Collins was.

Peter was already at the shop along with the other guys when I finally got there. Getting out of my truck, I headed inside. Instead of the guys being in the lounge area, they were all working hard in the conference room. The minute I walked in, seven sets of eyes looked my way. Peter stood and grabbed a laptop and said, "Take a seat, Ash, I've got something to show you."

Pulling the chair up beside him, I scooted closer to the long table and asked, "What do you have, Peter?"

170

Angling the laptop my way, the screen revealed a picture of Juliette getting inside a late model Rolls Royce. She was with an older gentleman that looked like he ate one too many donuts. Looking over to Peter, I asked, "Where is this at and who's the guy with Juliette?"

"I don't know for sure. These were the only images captured from the camera at the hotel. Without getting a clear shot of his face, it's going to be hard to identify him." Peter remarked.

"Wait, is that my truck?" I asked as I pointed to it on the screen.

"Yeah. You must have just missed them when you pulled up. Didn't you say that the check-in clerk said that one of the rooms was under a Walter Marlow?" Peter questioned.

"Yeah. She said that Sebastian had the room registered under him. She thought it was kind of odd, since he had the penthouse too. What are you thinking, Peter?" I knew just by the way he was looking that the wheels were spinning in his head.

171

"We got a tip on that trafficking ring. It may be related to the one in Nicaragua. The guy heading it was never found. This Walter character could be that guy," Peter stressed.

"Shit, Peter, if that's true, Juliette is in even more danger. We need to find her." I pleaded, pushing my chair away from the table as I stood. "I need to get the hell out of here and find her."

Before I could move from my spot, Peter had a hold of my arm. "Bro, you need to calm down. We got this. Sit and hear me out."

I took a deep breath and calmed my body. Sitting back in my chair, I listened to what Peter had to say. After listening to him and going over what he and the guys had planned, I had to admit it was a pretty good idea, and it made more sense than me trying to find her, half-cocked and pissed to the hilt.

~****~

It was late by the time I had left the shop. I wanted to stay later and help the guys work out the final details of the

172

plan, but Peter thought I was getting too emotionally involved. Damn straight I was. This plan revolved around Juliette, and I really cared about her, maybe even more than I was admitting. Grabbing a brew from the fridge, I sat on the couch and sipped it while staring out into the starry sky. Finishing the last of my brew, I could barely keep my eyes open.

When I got to bed, that all changed. The minute my head hit the pillow, my mind kept thinking about Juliette and the last time we were together. I wanted so badly to feel that again. I wanted to feel her soft skin pressed to me as I gently covered her mouth with mine. I was so lost in thought that I could even smell her scent. It was like cherry blossoms blowing in the wind. Pressing my eyes closed, I wanted her next to me so I imagined that she was. Her mouth was trailing feather-like kisses down my body. I could hear her soft voice whisper between each kiss. "I love kissing this," she said as she kissed my pounding heart. "And I love this," she added as she touched her lips lightly to my right eye and then to my left. "But most of all I love this," she breathed.

Just the thought of her saying those words made my cock throb with need. Reaching inside my sweat bottoms, I began stroking my thick member, seeing only Juliette. Her lips were so soft as the warmth of her mouth took me inside. I could feel the smooth gliding of her tongue over the tip before she slowly moved down my shaft to the base while she caressed my sac in her delicate hand. As I pumped deep inside her mouth, her soft whimpers of pleasure sounded. Juliette's movements began to increase and my cock grew to painful hardness. I continued pumping faster, harder, deeper until my control took off and I spilled with such fury that my body began to shudder with immense pleasure. Although the need to release was satisfied, the emptiness remained.

Pushing from the bed, I went to the bathroom and took a cold shower. This was the only way I was going to be able to simmer down the erection that was building again at the thought of having my cock inside her tight pussy.

I finally managed to fall asleep after my third shower, closing off every thought of Juliette. This wasn't an easy task to achieve, especially since she was the only thing that filled my thoughts over the past weeks.

As hard as it was to fall asleep, it was even harder to wake up. I must have hit the snooze button at least half a dozen times before I finally trudged out of bed. Walking to the kitchen, I prepared the coffee, making sure that I added

174

an extra scoop. In my opinion, caffeine was the breakfast of champs. Walking to the front door, I opened the door and took a deep breath of fresh air. Hearing my cell ring in the background, I hurried back inside to catch it before it went to voice mail. Picking it up from the counter, I just missed the call as the screen went black. Entering my password, I went to my recent calls to find that it had been Juliette who had called. With the small reel showing by the phone icon, I knew that she had left a message. With my cell to my ear, I began listening to the voice message. I played it over and over again, until it finally sunk in.

"Ash, please pick up. I may not be able to contact you again. Oh God, Ash, I'm so afraid. I don't even know where I am. Some sort of rundown mansion in the middle of nowhere. I... I'm so sorry, Ash, I should have told you everything. If we never see each other again, I want you to know one thing. I love you."

"What the hell do you think you're doing, you little wench?"

"Ash..."

Juliette was in danger and I had to find out where she was. The man's voice in the background was more than pissed off. I would never forget that voice as long as I lived. He had Juliette and as of right now, he was going to be a dead man.

Pouring the remainder of my coffee in a go-cup and filling it to the rim, I found Peter's number in my contacts and dialed his number while I hurried to my room to get dressed. "Peter, we need to rethink our plan. I think she is being kept in a rundown mansion on the outskirts of Manhattan. We need to find out if Walter Marlow has a property of this type. I'm heading to the shop. Should be there in thirty."

Before I gave Peter a chance to argue, I hung up and slipped on my jeans and a t-shirt. My boots were in the kitchen, so I grabbed them along with my coffee and headed down the stairs to the garage. It took me several tries to get the key in the ignition because my hand was shaking. Taking a deep breath, I was finally able to calm myself and start the engine.

I made it to the shop in record time. The stop lights were on my side and so was the traffic. As soon as I opened the door, I could see a very annoyed look on Peter's face as he was standing with his body leaning against the pool table.

"Would you like to explain to me what the hell is going on, Ash?" he asked in a heated tone.

"Sorry for the brusqueness of the call. I got a little anxious," I confessed.

"So, tell me what's going on," Peter said, pushing from the pool table and walking towards his office.

It was always my plan to bring Peter up to speed on what was going on and finding Juliette. When we got to Peter's office, I let it out. I told him everything from the beginning. He knew most of it already, but I thought if I went through it again, something would pop and we could figure out where Juliette was. Exhausted from my explanation, I took a seat and waited for Peter to boot up his computer. He had a lot more resources than I did, which meant there was somebody out there that he could reach out to.

I wasn't sure what he was looking at, but he had a confused look on his face. He picked up his landline and began dialing a number. It had to be someone he thought could help us. Whomever he called must have answered. Even though I could only hear Peter's side of the conversation, I knew that he was talking to someone by the name of Nick.

"I need this, Nick," Peter paused, presumably to wait for a response. "Yeah, his name is Walter Marlow. Call me back as soon as you find anything."

I watched Peter hang up the phone while looking at him with an inquisitive expression on my face. "So?" I asked.

"I think you may have been right about Mr. Marlow and Juliette being in more danger than we initially thought. Seems Mr. Marlow has been a very busy man. He has been purchasing rundown mansions outside of New York City. There are ten in total. I contacted Nick Winters from the county office. He has access to all the property records in New York. Maybe he can give us some insight on where Juliette is being held."

"Yeah, I gathered that, but how is he going to be able to do that?" I asked, confused.

"Because, my friend, he will be able to tell which of these dumps has an increase in utility usage. The more consumption, the more likely that the property is currently occupied," Peter explained.

It made perfect sense, especially since it was midsummer and the usage would be minimal. He couldn't occupy all of the homes at one time. In the meantime, I couldn't wait for Peter's friend to contact him back with the information. There was only one man who would know about Mr. Marlow, and that was Sebastian.

Standing, I started walking to the door when Peter stopped me. "Where are you going? Don't you want to wait until Nick calls back?"

"Call me on my cell with the information. There's somewhere I need to go," I admitted, but shared nothing else.

"Ash, if you are going where I think you are, don't do anything stupid," Peter warned.

Nodding my head, I left his office and headed out of the shop. Backing away from the building, I listened once again to the voice message that Juliette had left. I don't know why I was putting myself through this torture, but I had to hear her voice. God, I missed her so much. These feelings I had for her were much more than what they were twenty-four hours ago. After hearing her say, *'I love you,'* those were going to be the only words she would hear from me the minute when I took her in my arms.

Parking across the street, I walked over to the Collins Building. As I stood in front of the elevator door, I controlled my fear of getting into that elevator and just stepped inside. Using my breathing exercises, I managed to tone down my anxiety until the car stopped on the thirty-fifth floor. When the doors opened, I was grateful that Bambi with the fake tits was away from her perch, which allowed me to walk into Sebastian's office unannounced.

Pushing open the door, I was greeted with his icy glare as he laid his expensive pen on his desk. With the clench of his jaw, he seethed, "What do you want?"

"I want to know where the fuck Juliette is!" I cursed as I moved closer to his desk, my knuckles white from my tight fists.

"What makes you think I know anything, or would even tell you if I did?" Sebastian chuckled, his mouth twitched with amusement.

"I know all about Walter Marlow. Your contract with Juliette. Now where the fuck is she?" I snapped with disgust as I stepped closer to him, ready to wipe that shit eating grin from his face.

"Your time is up, Mr. Jacobs," Sebastian paused, looking to his office door where two security guards were now standing. "Gentlemen, just in time. Mr. Jacobs was just leaving. If he enters the building again have him arrested for trespassing."

This was far from over. One way or another I was going to find out what he was hiding. As the two security guards escorted me out of the building, I noticed a chubby fellow getting out of a late model Cadillac. I didn't know what it was about this man, but there was something familiar about him. His head was lowered and he looked as though he hadn't bathed in some time. Not even the expensive-looking suit he wore could better his appearance.

Pulling a dollar bill from my pocket, I walked up to him and asked, "Excuse me, sir. Do you have change for a dollar?"

The man looked up to me and smiled with tobacco-stained teeth. Digging in his pocket, he pulled out some loose change and began counting it as he picked out a couple of quarters and five dimes. Handing it over to me, he said in a gruff voice, probably caused from years of smoking, "Here you go. Don't spend it all in one place?"

I didn't catch the humor, but there was something definitely familiar about him. I just couldn't put my finger on it. I put the change in my pocket and watched him walk inside the building. Going with my gut, I pulled out my phone and took a picture of his plate before heading back to my truck. As I got inside, I noticed a yellow slip under my wiper. I was in such a hurry to get inside the building that I neglected to deposit some money into the meter. Opening the glove box, I threw it inside, adding it to the collection of parking tickets I had already had. I never really had to worry about them. Peter had an in with the NYPD and the parking tickets were waived.

About halfway back to the shop, it dawned on me what was so familiar about that guy. It was his voice. Whipping a U-turn, I headed back to the Collins building to wait for the guy to come out. It didn't matter that I had broken all of the traffic laws in order to get there, because by the time I arrived, the Cadillac was already gone.

CHAPTER SIXTEEN
Juliette

Somehow, I managed to fall asleep in the lumpy bed that was in the bedroom I was escorted to. Mr. Marlow said that it was the best room in the house and had all the comforts of a fancy hotel. "Fancy hotel, my ass," I said out loud as I tried to work the kinks out of my neck. At least I was thankful for one thing, the bedding was clean. Scooting to the edge of the bed from the middle, since the middle had the least amount of lumps, I got up and headed to the bathroom to pee.

When I arrived early this morning, all I wanted to do was to cuddle up and go to sleep. I never made it to the bathroom, so when I switched on the light, my eyes flared with disgusted. The bathroom wasn't fit for a dog. The tub was stained with rust from where the water must have continually run. There was also a wide ring around the rim, which I was pretty sure never saw a drop of cleaner. And the sink was in the same condition. I was almost afraid to touch anything for fear that I was going to catch something. I guess for every down side there is an up side. At least there were clean towels on the vanity.

Turning on the water in the sink, it ran brown. I waited for a minute until the water turned clear before I splashed a handful on my face. Drying my face off with the rough towel, I walked over to the tub and turned the nozzle to the hot water, and then the cold, and waited for the water to turn clear before I set the plug in the drain. When the water was just below the stained ring, I turned it off and began taking off my clothes, which wasn't much, considering what I came with.

Stepping inside the tub, I was careful not to touch the sides. There was a bar of soap that appeared to be unused in the dish, which I used to clean myself. Having spent all the time in the tub that I could stand, I got out and dried my body, wrapping the damp towel around me for coverage while I hunted for something to wear.

Opening the door to the closet, there wasn't much inside by way of clothing, but there were plenty of nightgowns and robes, most of which looked to be very expensive. Looking through the assortment, I decided on a conservative black nightgown with a matching robe. Slipping it on, it didn't surprise me in the least that it fit perfectly. Drawing my eyes to the floor, I saw that for every nightgown there were a pair of fancy slippers to match. Once again, I picked the most conservative pair and slipped them on, again fitting perfectly.

With only a nightgown and a robe on, I needed to see if I could find some underwear and maybe even a bra. Opening every drawer in the dresser, I came up empty. *"What kind of sicko is he?"* I thought to myself as I closed the last drawer.

With nothing left to do, I sat back down on the bed until either Mr. Marlow or one of his servants came to get me. As I was sitting there lost in thought, I remembered the one thing that might help me get out of here. Walking over to the dusty red velvet chair in the corner of the room, I picked up my trench coat and dug inside the pocket for my cell phone. Pulling up the screen, I only had fifteen percent battery life left. It was just enough for what I needed to do.

Ash was at the top of my favorite contacts so it didn't take me long to dial him. The call went to voicemail and the only thing I could do was leave a message. Before I could finish the message, my phone was ripped from my hand.

Turning to face the one person that made my stomach churn, I saw the evil in his eyes before he asked, "What the hell do you think you're doing, you little wench?"

I yelled one last time for Ash, but I knew it was too late. My only chance of getting out of here was destroyed, and with a backhand to the face I was down. With a look of conviction on his face, Mr. Marlow hissed, "You will never see him again," before he left the room, slamming the door behind him.

~****~

I must have cried myself to sleep, because when I woke up, the sun was beginning to set. I also knew by the sound my stomach was making that I hadn't eaten for nearly twenty-four hours. Pushing to my feet, I walked over to the door and turned the knob. Either Mr. Marlow forgot to lock the door or he was testing me. It didn't matter to me either way. I knew that if I didn't try and get out of this place, I was surely going to die here.

Cracking the door an inch, I put my ear to the crack to see if I could hear anything going on from the other side. When I was met with only silence, I opened it a little further until I was able to peek outside into the long hallway. There was no one in sight. Running back to the bed, I grabbed my slippers and slowly headed down the long hallway in the direction that I came when Mr. Marlow brought me here.

This was too easy. It had to be a test. I was already down the marble staircase and almost to the front door with no sign of anyone. Tiptoeing along, I heard a noise coming from the other room. All I could think about was getting caught. I began trying all the doors near me to find a place to hide. Every door I tried was locked. The voices were getting nearer and I was running out of options. Trying the last door, it opened and I slipped inside. I must have slipped inside a closet because it was pitch black and smelt like someone had died.

Putting my ear against the door and concentrating on the voices instead of the smell, I heard one of the men say, "He has gone to meet with Mr. Collins. He won't be back for another hour. He wants us to wait until he gets back to feed Miss Daniels and has advised us to feed her only one slice of bread and one glass of water. He needs her to have some strength for what he has planned for her this evening." I heard the man chuckle at his lame humor.

As soon as the voices were gone, I knew that I was in the clear. Even though I knew I had an hour, it wasn't much time to get far away from here. I slowly opened the door to the closet and looked around for any sign of the men. With my slippers in my hand, I quietly walked to the front door as quickly as possible without making a sound. Pulling the door open, it began to creak, taking my breath away. I thought for sure that I was caught, but no one ever came. They must have been far enough away not to hear the screeching sound.

As soon as I hit the outside, I pulled the slippers on and ran. I didn't even bother closing the front door as I left, which was probably a mistake. The cobblestone drive was a killer on my feet, but I knew that I had to keep going. Reaching the end of the drive, I turned to the left and headed down the paved road. Watching for oncoming cars, I steered clear of them by lying down in the embankment until they passed and were out of sight. The last thing I wanted was to run into that piece of shit coming back.

I knew that it had to have been close to an hour since I ran from the mansion. It was only a matter of time before he spotted me if I continued walking down this road. While I was thinking the best thing to do was to take one of the side roads, a car appeared from the other direction. I thought for sure it was Mr. Marlow's servants coming to look for me. But when the car stopped and the driver rolled down the window, I knew it wasn't them. A young girl who couldn't have been much older than me was sitting behind the wheel.

I continued walking until she asked, "Hey, do you need a ride?"

Turning towards her, I said, "Yeah, that would be great," as I began walking to the passenger side of the car.

Once inside, she turned down the radio and asked, "Where were you heading to, dressed like that?"

"It's a long story, but do you think you could take me to Maplewood?" I asked.

"Today is your lucky day, I have to go through Maplewood. My folks live in Springfield. I'm visiting them for summer break. I'm Maddy, by the way," she said, holding out her hand.

"I'm Juliette," I replied.

While Maddy was driving, there wasn't one minute that passed that she didn't talk. Most of the time I wasn't even listening to her. My thoughts were focused on the mess I was currently in. I tried several times to chime in on the conversation, but was stopped by something totally different than what she was talking about to begin with. In one breath, she was talking about the history class she took and how she thought the professor was hot and in the next she was talking about whether or not she should color her hair pink.

I couldn't have been more ready to step out of the car by the time she pulled up to my place. I wanted her to wait while I went inside to get her some money for gas, but she insisted that it was no problem and on the way to where she was going anyway.

Waving her goodbye, I took a deep breath of relief and went inside the house. God, it felt good to be home. I knew I couldn't stay here, but I desperately needed a shower and a change of clothes. But more than anything, I needed Ash.

~****~

I think I must have died and gone to heaven. Even though my bathtub was nothing like the one at the Four Seasons, it was mine and it was clean. My whole body was engulfed in mounds and mounds of bubbles. The scent of vanilla filled the room, giving me a relaxing tranquil atmosphere. With my ear buds in, I was in absolute heaven.

Knowing that I needed to get going, I drained the water and began drying off. When I opened the bathroom door, the smell was almost unbearable. Something was burning. I quickly slipped on my clothes to check out what was going on. Opening the door, I could see that there was a fire in the living room. The couch and the curtains were in flames. Hurrying to the kitchen, I grabbed the small fire extinguisher that I put inside the pantry closet and pulled the pin from the handle. Aiming it towards the fire, I squeezed the handle until the white foam came out. It didn't matter how hard I tried to douse the fire, it was too much for the extinguisher to handle.

Throwing it to the floor. I ran to the front door to escape the inferno. I kept pulling and tugging on the door, but it wouldn't open. I decided to try the back door. I needed to get out of this house before the fire consumed everything inside, including me. Turning the knob to the door, just like the front door, it wouldn't open. I was beginning to panic. There were four windows in the house, but the front window wasn't an escape option since it was covered in flames. Since I was already in the kitchen, I moved the light sheer curtains covering the window back, only to find that the window wouldn't open. "What the hell!" I screamed in a panic.

Going to the bedroom, it was the same thing. Even the small window in the bathroom wouldn't open. I couldn't understand what was going on. The first thing I checked when I bought the house was that all the windows worked properly. About ready to give up, I remembered that the basement had a couple of windows. As I opened the door leading to the downstairs, the lights began to flicker until they went completely out. The fire must have caused a short in the wiring. Frantically, I began opening drawer after drawer until I found the flashlight.

As I headed down the steps, I could feel the smoke getting thicker and thicker. I knew if I didn't hurry and get out of the house, it would kill me. Reaching the bottom of the steps, I shined the light at the window. Stepping up on a box, I tried to push it open, but it was stuck. My guess was from not being used. I wished I had taken the time to check it as well. Looking around, I found a metal pipe. Hopping from the box, I ran over to grab it. The smoke was unbearable and I could feel it begin to creep inside my lungs. It was getting harder to breathe. I began feeling weak and could feel my body fall to the concrete. I knew then it was too late.

CHAPTER SEVENTEEN

Ash

I could have kicked myself in the ass for not sticking around until the guy in the Cadillac left. Juliette was in my mind so much that I couldn't even think straight. I needed to get my head together. Circling the block, I decided the best thing to do was to head back to my place and rethink everything that I knew to be fact. Hopefully by then I would hear from Peter.

Driving through the Holland Tunnel to the I-78 Express, my chest began to tighten. I had never had this feeling before. I knew something was wrong. I could feel it in my body. Stepping on the gas, I hurried down the highway, weaving in and out of cars like a madman. Hitting the main road to Maplewood, I almost lost control of my truck as I took the corner a little faster than I should have.

Turning down the dirt road to my house, I couldn't believe what I saw. There was smoke coming from the road where Juliette lived. Stepping on the gas pedal, I made a sharp turn, causing the back end of the truck to fishtail. The closer I got to her house the more I could see the flames billowing out of the roof and the front window. My heart sank.

Jumping out of the truck. I tried to get as close as I could to the house. Something wasn't right. The front door had been secured from the outside with a two-by-four. *Why would the house be locked up this way?* Heading around the side of the house, I could see that Juliette's bedroom window and her bathroom window were also secured with a board. There was only one reason the house would be boarded up in this manner. It was either to keep someone from getting in or someone from getting out. There was no way I would be able to get inside the house by trying to remove the boards. Jogging around to the backside of the house, the back door was also secured with a two-by-four. *"What the fuck,"* I thought to myself.

Scratching my head, I tried to figure out how I was going to get inside. Frustrated, I kicked the head off of a bumblebee lawn ornament and watched it roll to a stop in front of one of the basement windows. Noticing that there were no boards on it, I hurried over to it and crouched down.

196

I couldn't get it open. Cleaning off a small area of the glass with my hand, there was a faint light on. Looking around the yard, I tried to find something hard that I could use to break the window.

Finding a large rock, I threw it against the glass and watched as the glass shattered into a million pieces onto the dirt. Smoke began seeping out. It wasn't as black as the smoke coming from the roof, which told me that the fire hadn't reached that part of the house yet.

Carefully, I removed the rest of the glass and went through the open hole, feet first. When I got inside, the thickness of the smoke just about knocked me over. Keeping my hand over my mouth, I made my way over to where the light was shining. There was a small body on the ground next to a flashlight. As I got closer, I saw that it was Juliette.

Taking her in my arms, I lifted her head and said, "Juliette."

Her face was pale and her body was limp like a Raggedy Ann doll. Putting my finger to her pulse, I could feel that she was still alive. Picking her up, I headed back to the window that I came through. There was no way I was going to be able to get her out this way. Setting her down for a minute, I walked up the stairs and felt the door for heat. The door was warm, but not hot. I had to take a chance that the fire hadn't reached the kitchen yet. Opening it slowly, all I could see was smoke and not red flames. Going back down, I took Juliette once again in my arms and climbed the stairs two at a time.

As I got to the back door, my will to save her took over. With everything I had, I kicked the door over and over until it flew open. With Juliette in my arms, I took her away from the inferno and laid her gently on the hard ground. There was still a pulse, even though it was faint. I tilted her head back and opened her mouth and began giving her breaths. At first there was nothing, but then she began coughing. I held her next to me and said, "I thought I lost you."

Her eyes began to flutter and she tried to speak. "You found me," she finally whispered softly

"Let's get out of here," I replied, picking her up and taking her over to the truck.

I carefully laid her on the back seat where I knew she would be more comfortable until I got her back to my place. Sliding behind the wheel, I looked back to her to make sure she was still okay. Her eyes had fallen closed, but the rise and fall of her chest let me know that she was still breathing. Pulling my phone from my pocket, I dialed 911 and let the dispatcher know to send out the fire department to Juliette's address. I knew they wouldn't be able to save the house, but at least they would be able to stop it from spreading into the wooded area and down the road to my place.

~****~

After I got Juliette in the house and situated in my bed, I headed to the kitchen to call Peter. I hadn't heard back from him regarding Walter Marlow, and I needed to let him know that I had Juliette. Dialing his number, I took a beer from the fridge as I waited for him to answer.

"Please tell me that you aren't in any trouble?" Peter answered.

"You need to have a little faith," I began. "But there is a problem. Juliette's house was set on fire. It's nothing but a heap of ashes. Someone wanted her dead, but didn't pull it off. They boarded up the house tighter than security at the Fort Knox."

"So, are you saying that Juliette was in the house?" Peter asked, confused.

"Yeah, I don't know all of the details, but she's safe now. She's here at my house and I'm not going to let her out of my sight."

"If she tells you anything, let me know. We might have a lead on where Mr. Marlow is living. I'll call you back as soon as we know for sure," Peter declared

Placing my cell on the counter, I finished drinking my beer before grabbing another. Walking over to the floor-to-ceiling windows in the living room, I looked out to see that Juliette's house was still burning. I could hear the sirens in the distance, which let me know that they had arrived. I felt a tightening in my gut as I thought about Juliette and how much she wanted to make something of that old house.

It had to have been at least a couple of hours, if not more, that I had been looking out the window. At least I didn't see the flames rising in between the trees anymore.

The only thing left was a cloud of smoke in the distance where Juliette's house once stood. As I turned to walk away from the window and check on her, I saw her small frame standing a few feet in front of me.

Walking into the light, she had a blanket wrapped around her like a child that had been woken from a bad dream. She moved slowly to the large windows and looked out to where her house used to be. Coming up behind her, I wrapped my arms around her and held her body close to mine. I could feel her body tremble with sadness as she watched her dream taken away. Turning her body away from the destruction, I lifted her chin and said, "It isn't the end, Juliette. We will find who did this and they will pay. I promise."

Leaning her head against my chest, I could hear the pain in her voice. It nearly broke my heart. "It will never be okay. He will find me. I will never find true happiness."

Picking her up, I took a seat on the couch and pulled her body close to mine. She nuzzled her head just under my chin. I wanted to help her, but the only way I was going to be able to do that was to know the truth. "Juliette, you need to trust me. I need to know everything if I am going to be able to help you."

"I know," she mumbled. "I just don't want you to hate me."

Putting her at arm's length, I looked into her beautiful green eyes and confessed, "Not in a million years could I ever hate you. I care for you so much that it kills me to see you this way. Whoever did this needs to pay."

Snuggling against me, I heard her speak in a soft voice. "I've made such a mess of my life." Looking up at me she hesitated for a moment before she began again. "When I was eighteen, I got caught shoplifting a very expensive lipstick. I don't know why I took it. I just really wanted it. The lady who owned the store said I was trespassing and that I broke into her store. It was my word against hers. The door was open and I walked in. There was nobody around so I thought I could take the lipstick and leave before anyone noticed."

"What does this have to do with Sebastian and the contract?" I asked.

202

"Somehow Sebastian found out about it. He came to the police station and paid my bail. He said that he could take care of everything and that I wouldn't have to spend any time in jail. He offered me a deal. That was when I signed the contract you found. He promised that nothing bad would happen to me and that he would take care of me. Even offered to put me through college," she confessed before continuing. "I did everything he asked. He introduced me to so many men, and he told me all I had to do was please them in any way they wanted. I had never been with a man before, Ash."

I could see the torment in her eyes. Sebastian took her innocence for his own personal gain. I felt my blood boil just thinking about what he did to her. Stroking my hand through her hair, I needed to hear the rest, no matter how disgusting it was. "It's okay, Juliette."

"Then I was introduced to Mr. Marlow. The minute I saw him, I knew he was a bad man. He did things to me that no one should have to ever endure. I will never forget the first time with him. Sebastian taught me many things, but he never prepared me for what that asshole did to me," she cried out as she sucked in a breath. "It didn't matter how many times I told him 'No,' he kept going. And then... Sebastian

203

did the unthinkable. He sold me to him. Just like that, he handed me over like I was nothing more than another business deal."

"You don't need to say anything more, Jules," I whispered.

Lowering my head, I kissed her on the forehead and placed my hand on her cheek. Her eyes were filled with such pain. I was sure she knew how I felt about her and what she meant to me. I couldn't care less about her past and the men she had been subjected to. All I cared about was keeping her safe. Lifting her chin, I looked into her emerald eyes and said, "I'm never going to let anything happen to you."

Her lips met mine and I pulled her even closer to my body, kissing her deeply. A sweet, breathless whimper escaped her lips. I lifted her in the air and positioned her body so that it was straddling mine. Lifting her arms above her head, I removed the t-shirt I had given her to wear. As I pulled it over her head, her sweet scent filled my head and my need for her took over. Breaking the kiss, I lowered my head and took a hardened nipple between my lips and gently caressed it with my tongue. Juliette's head fell back, pushing her taut bud even closer to my lips.

204

Unable to hold back my aching desire, I moved her off of my lap and laid her carefully along the couch. Pulling down her lacy panties, I consumed more of her sweetness. Placing one knee on the couch, I balanced my body close to hers with my foot that was still on the floor. Running my hands down her silky skin, I lifted her legs higher so that her butt was in the air and off the couch. Having the access that I needed, I began kissing her on the stomach, dipping my tongue inside her navel before moving on to her cleanly shaven mound.

Drawing her near, I slid my tongue down her clit to her folds, where I found her wet with the sweetest honey I had ever tasted. Her fingers began running through my hair as I continued my assault on her clit. Dipping a finger inside, I could feel the warmth of her channel as I began pumping in and out of her. I could feel her walls tighten, pulling my finger deeper inside. Finding her special spot, I placed my finger along the rough area, rubbing it slowly. Her hips began to buck, moving with the motion of my finger. Sucking her swollen nub, I bit it lightly, causing the juices within her to spill on my finger. Removing my hand, I glided it up her body and lapped up the remaining nectar with my tongue.

Needing to satisfy my need for her, I quickly unzipped my pants and pushed them down my legs. Setting my raging arousal free, I slowly glided inside her warmth. The sensation of being enveloped and held tightly was unlike anything I had felt before. With every thrust, her walls clinched down and began milking me. I could tell she was close to her own release as her hips began to rock faster. As much as I wanted to take this slow and savor every minute with her, my will to control my release was beginning to lose out. Juliette moved her hand down between us and reached for the base of my sac. Never had a woman done that before. It felt so fucking good that my desire won out and I spilled like Niagara Falls deep inside her.

We remained on the couch for a moment, feeling the weight of all the pain being lifted from inside us. I could feel Juliette's warm breath on my chest. She had been through so much in the past weeks. Never was there a woman as strong as she was. To be so young and trusting and then to be taken advantage of, knowing there was no way out, had to have been the hardest thing for her to go through. But no more. She was never going to go through that again. I didn't care what it took.

Careful not to wake her, I slid out from under her, grabbed the throw blanket, and wrapped it around her. Lifting her off of the couch, I carried her back to my room where I knew she would be more comfortable. Feeling her hand come up to my face, her eyes opened and a sense of security fell upon her face. Kissing her lightly on the forehead, I could no longer keep in the feelings I had for her. In a soft whisper, I confessed, "I love you, Juliette Daniels."

CHAPTER EIGHTEEN
Juliette

It didn't matter that my life was pretty much over. I was still happy and my secret was out in the open. Ash still wanted me after I told him everything. He even told me that he loved me. This was something I hadn't heard for a very long time. Rolling over on my side, I watched as Ash's chest rose with every breath he took. I could stare at him for hours and still not get enough of him. Kissing him on his chest, I felt him take in a deep breath. With one hand on his tight abs and the other tucked under his head, he turned his head slightly and opened his eyes.

I had never really taken a good look at them, but they were gorgeous. They had light specks of gray near his pupil that extended to the outside. And with his dark lashes, it was no wonder he captured my heart.

Kissing him tenderly on the lips, I slowly pushed away from him and said, "I need to take a shower."

Before I was off of the bed, he had me in his arms, carrying me to the bathroom. I guess he decided that he needed to take a shower too. Setting me down, he opened the glass door to the shower and turned the water on. When the temperature was where it needed to be, we both got in and took in the warmth the water offered as it cascaded down our bodies. Ash grabbed the sponge and put a generous amount of body wash on it. Placing it on my back, he began rubbing it lightly across my my skin as his lips fell to my neck.

My mind was reeling with pleasure as he continued kissing me lightly on the neck. He lowered the sponge to my lower back before sliding it down my butt and in between my legs. With his breath so close to my ear, he whispered softly, "Spread those gorgeous legs, baby."

I spread my legs without hesitation as he continued to gently rub the soft sponge between them. My head fell back against his chest as he moved the sponge to my clit and began making slow circular movements. The pleasure he was giving me was so intense, I couldn't take it any more. In a heated breath, I moaned, "Ash, please."

He knew exactly what I wanted. Dropping the sponge to the floor, he twisted my body so that I was facing him.

Lifting my leg off the tile floor, he took hold of his impressive cock and guided it inside me. As his hand held me in place, he began pumping his shaft deeper and deeper. I could feel him fill me as his cock continued to pulsate between my walls.

Letting go of my hips, his hands ventured to my breasts, where he took each nipple between his fingers and began rubbing and pinching them. With the added sensation, my body shook, releasing the desire I had for him. Giving me one last thrust, I felt the tremor of his body, letting me know that he was also met with his desire.

An hour later, we were both finally dressed and on our way to the kitchen to satisfy the appetite we had worked up in the shower. As I got the coffee ready, Ash was busy pulling various items from the fridge. Taking a seat at the bar, I watched as Ash worked his magic with the ingredients in front of him, but mostly I was looking at his ass as he turned to drop the chopped vegetables in the pan that was on the stove. This was something that I would never get tired of.

Needing a distraction, I decide to do something constructive, like set the table. Pushing from my seat, I rounded the bar and open the cupboard where the plates were located. My eyes drifted back over to Ash, taking in his perfection.

~****~

I offered to clean up the dishes while Ash took a call on his cell. He wandered into the living room so I wasn't really sure who he was talking to. If I had to take a guess, I would say that it had to be one of the guys he worked with. After placing the last dish in the dishwasher, I walked over to where he was. His shoulder was leaning against the long window while he gazed out. Stepping up behind him, I wrapped my arms around his waist as he finished his call. I could barely see over his shoulder to see what he was looking at. The sky was still hazy from the fire.

Letting him go, I moved beside him so I could get a better look. Thinking about what I had lost, my eyes began to fill with tears. My breath hitched and the words that came from inside were barely recognizable. "It's gone, Ash. The one thing that I could call my own is gone."

Ash pulled me close and wrapped his comforting arms around me. Holding me tight, he kissed the top of the head and replied, "I want you here with me, Jules. There's one thing that you will always own."

I looked up at him with confusion and asked,"What's that, Ash?"

Placing his hand on my cheek, he looked at me and said, "Me."

It was the most sincere thing that anyone had ever said to me. My heart was filled with happiness that he wanted me as much as I wanted him. At that moment, I knew that everything was going to be okay. Taking my hand, Ash led me over to the couch and pulled me to his lap as he sat down. His expression got serious as he rubbed the back of my hand. Looking at him with concern, I asked, "What's wrong, Ash?"

"I want you to come to the shop with me. We need to talk to Peter about what you shared with me. Do you think you're up to it?"

Nodding my head "Yes," I stood and went to the guest bedroom where I knew my shoes would be. When I got back to the living area, Ash was waiting for me with his hands in his pockets, looking as gorgeous as ever. When I smiled at him, he mimicked mine with one of his own. "Are you ready?" he asked.

"Yeah, let's go," I replied, following behind him.

As we drove away from Ash's house, I kept thinking about what Ash said. He wanted me to be with him. To live with him in his home. I really didn't have much of a choice at that point, seeing as how my home was burnt to the ground. Reaching the short road leading to my house. I looked over to Ash and asked, "Can we stop at the house for a minute?"

Ash placed his hand on my thigh and squeezed it lightly. "Are you sure you want to do that?" he questioned with a hint of concern in his tone.

"I have to at least look, Ash. There may be something that can be salvaged," I responded.

When he got to the house, the only thing left of my house were a few boards that managed to survive the fire. Opening the door, I climbed out of the truck and walked up to where the wooden porch use to be. Before I could take a step further, Ash was right behind me. His voice was stern as he warned, "Don't go in there, Jules. The floor doesn't look very solid."

Looking down at the floor, he was right. The floor was black. Even though it was still intact, the fire could have weakened the boards and I could have ended up in the basement. It didn't matter that I couldn't get inside. As far as I could see there wasn't anything left of the house or of my things. It would take too long to try and get to the basement, and we really didn't have the time at the moment.

Backing away from the porch, I walked back over to the truck and got in. Ash got in as well and started the engine. As he backed away from the house, all I wanted was to know who had done this. Ash must have known what I was thinking. "We will find out who did this, Jules, and they will pay."

~****~

Ash parked his truck next to a fancy-looking Camaro. Getting out of the truck, I realized that it was the first time I had been to the place where he worked. It was also going to be the first time that I would be meeting all of the guys. Ash

214

opened the door to the shop, and right away I was greeted by four tall, extremely hot muscular guys.

As I followed Ash, he began introducing them to me one by one. "Guys, I want you to meet my girl, Juliette Daniels." Ash paused for a moment and waited for the guys to say hello. Pointing at the first alpha-male, he said, "Jules, I want you to meet Cop. His real name is Vince Coppoletti, but we call him Cop for short."

Pointing to the next guy, he smiled, "This here is Lou Gainer."

With a tip of his head, Lou replied, "Ma'am."

Continuing his introductions, I was introduced to Sylvester Capelli, who went by the name of 'Sly,' and Mike Chavez. Ash went on to explain how all of them served together in Iraq. I could tell that they were all very close by the way they joked with each other and carried on. While I was listening to their conversation, another alpha-male type walked into the room. Ash looked over to him, then took my hand and led me to where he was standing.

"Jules, this is Peter Hewitt. He's the one who owns Jagged Edge Security. He is one of the best men I have ever known."

Holding out my hand, I said, "It's nice to meet you."

"Ryan and Josh are already in the conference room. We have a lot to go over with the new developments," Peter remarked.

Leading the way, we all followed Peter into the conference room. Just like he said, two men were already seated at the long table, engrossed in whatever they were looking at on their laptops. Clearing his voice, Peter said, "Guys, this is Juliette Daniels." As they poked their heads up for a moment, Peter continued the introductions. "Juliette, this is Ryan Hyatt and his younger brother Josh."

Waving my hand to them, I replied with a simple, "Hi."

As everyone took their seats, Ash and I walked towards the front of the table, with Peter sitting at the head of the table and the rest of the guys in the remaining chairs. Peter began explaining the information he had found out.

"I've been in touch with our contact at the FBI concerning human trafficking for sex. It seems Sebastian Collins as well as Walter Marlow are persons of interest."

Looking over to Ash with confusion, I looked back at Peter and asked, "What did you just say?"

"We know about your relationship with Mr. Collins and Mr. Marlow, Juliette," Peter claimed.

Rising to my feet, I could feel a tightness in my chest. I felt like the one person I trusted just took everything we had and shit all over it. Opening the door to the conference room, I hurried to the front door. I knew Ash was right behind me the minute I heard his voice. "Jules, wait, let me explain."

"What is there to explain, Ash? Now everyone knows about my pathetic life. How could you? We were going to do this together," I hissed.

Stopping my movements, Ash tugged on my arm and pulled me next to him. "It wasn't like that, Jules. When I read the contract and saw Sebastian's name, I had Peter run a check on him. This was way before you told me everything. They are here to help you, not judge you. Please, Jules, help

217

us figure this out and put those assholes behind bars for what they did. Our guess is you aren't the only girl who fell into their plans."

"Do you really think there are other girls?" I asked, pushing my anger aside.

"I know there are. Come back to the conference room and listen to what Peter found out," Ash pleaded.

When we re-entered the room, we saw Peter had posted some pictures on a white board. One was of the old mansion that Mr. Marlow had taken me to. Unable to hold back, I shouted, "I know that house! I was there, before I escaped."

CHAPTER NINETEEN

Ash

When Jules shouted that she had been in that house, I knew we had a lead. Looking over to Peter, he had this confused look on his face. Turning to Juliette, he asked, "Are you sure Juliette? Sebastian Collins owns this house and if Walter Marlow took you there, it confirms that they are working together."

"I will never forget that house. That is where he took me. I would bet my life on it," she swore.

"Did you see anything while you were there?" Peter asked.

"Other than it was a dump, not really. I do remember that almost all of the doors were locked on the main floor. I almost didn't make it out of there," Juliette answered with a disgusted look on her face.

"We think that Sebastian and Walter may be keeping the women they are getting ready to sell inside that house. After Nick, my friend from the city office, did some research, he concluded that it was the only house that had any utility usage," Peter explained, his eyes on Juliette as he pointed at the rundown mansion. "We need to get someone inside to make sure. That's where you come in."

I could tell by the look on Juliette's face that she didn't know what it was exactly that Peter was asking of her. I was totally against it and recommended that we send Nikki inside. Peter argued that there wasn't enough time to get the bait set and Juliette was our only chance.

Peter began explaining what the plan was, giving her a scenario as to what could happen if the plan went sour. The first thing he needed to do was make sure that the abducted women were inside. If they weren't there, then there were still nine other properties that needed to be checked out. With everything he had said, she still wanted to help, even knowing that if they found out what she was up to, she could end up dead. All Juliette wanted was to make sure Sebastian and Walter were locked up for life.

Driving back to my place, all I could think about was the plan that Peter put into place and what he expected of Juliette. I knew that there was always a risk with every mission we had, but to have someone you loved involved, it was an even greater risk. Diverting my eyes to Juliette, I said to her, "Jules, you don't have to do this. We can find another way."

When she moved her eyes from the road to me, her expression said it all. She didn't have to say anything for me to know that she was going to do this. "Ash, I have to do this. Just like you said, they needed to pay for what they did. They took everything from me. All I want is to give them what they deserve. I want them to know what it feels like to lose everything."

If anyone deserved to be righted for what those two men had done, it was Jules. I wasn't sure how many other women had suffered under their hands, but they deserved justice as well. Letting her know that I understood, I took hold of her hand and squeezed it gently.

There was still enough of the day left that we decided to go over to her place and see if there was anything that we could find that she could save. Turning down the short road

221

to her house, I made a half circle and backed up as close as I could to the porch. Juliette got out and began surveying the damage. My guess was that she was trying to figure out a way to get inside without falling through the floor.

Standing beside her, I took in the mess and figured out that the best way to get inside was to try and go through the basement. Going to the side of the house, I saw the broken window that I entered. I thought it would be better if I went in first, just in case the house was unstable. As I crawled through the window, the strong smell of burnt wood filled my senses. Looking above me to the ceiling, I could see the fire hadn't made it to the floor joists or the underside of the floor. This was a good indication the floor above was sturdy enough to walk on. Walking up the steps, I tried pushing open the door, but something must have fallen against it during the fire.

Crawling back through the window, Juliette was standing outside waiting for me. Giving me her hand, she tried to help through the window. This was the cutest thing ever. I wasn't sure why she thought her one-hundred-twenty pound body could pull my two-hundred pound body from the window.

Once I got to my feet, I brushed off my pants and said, "I think the floor is strong enough to walk on. Just in case, let me check it out first."

Jules nodded in agreement as we walked back to the front of the house. Grabbing a piece of wood from the burnt debris, I checked to make sure it was strong enough by stabbing it into the ground. Satisfied that it would work, I headed to where the porch used to be. When I got to front doorway, I began poking the wood with the stick to make sure it was stable. With every step I took Juliette was right behind me. While I poked, she looked around to see if she could see anything that resembled any of her personal things.

By the time we had finished searching the mess, Juliette's hands were covered in black soot from picking up whatever she thought was something important. I had never met a person more determined to find at least one thing that was worth saving. Taking what little she had found, I placed in the bed of the truck for her.

As we got inside the truck, my cell phone rang. Looking down at the screen, it was Peter. I wasn't sure why he would be calling, unless he had some more information for me. Swiping the screen, I answered, "What's up, Peter?"

"Are you with Juliette?" he asked.

"Yeah, let me put you on speaker," I responded.

"The fire marshal did a sweep of the Juliette's house. They didn't find anything that would indicate that the fire was intentionally started. They are ruling that the house probably had faulty wiring, considering how old it was. I'm really sorry, Juliette. I was hoping they would find something."

"Wait, what about the boarded windows and doors?" I asked.

"Nothing, bro. Whoever did this was very smart and knew exactly what they were doing," Peter replied before he continued. "We may not be able to tie the fire to Mr. Collins or Mr. Marlow, but we will get them."

This was not what I wanted to hear, and by the look on Juliette's face, neither did she. I guess it would have been too easy to pin this on them. Just like Peter said, whoever did this knew exactly what they were doing.

I backed the truck in the garage like I always did. Juliette didn't move from her spot. I knew she was disappointed by Peter's news. Taking the key from the ignition, I rounded the front of the truck and opened her door. With a tear escaping her eye, she looked at me and said, "He can't win. This needs to end or I will never be free of him."

She was right, this did need to end. She had been through enough. Pressing my lips to hers, I whispered with conviction, "It will end. I'll make sure of it."

~****~

"How about we take a break?" I said to Jules as I set down a crystal vase.

"Okay, how about I fix us some lunch?" she suggested.

We had spent most of the morning cleaning and polishing the items she was able to save from the fire. It wasn't helping her to forget about the fire, but at least it was keeping her busy. Finishing up, we both stood and headed inside the house. It was another hot day and the only thing I wanted was to cool my body off. Opening up the fridge, I grabbed two brews and popped the tops. Jules was busy making us sandwiches, so I decided to check with the guys to see if Hawk and Isabelle had made it in safely. Snagging my phone off of the counter, I dialed Peter's number and waited for him to answer.

"Hey, bro," he answered with enthusiasm.

"By the sound of your voice, Hawk and Isabelle must have made it in," I replied.

"Yeah, we are all at the shop catching up. Why don't you and Juliette come down?"

"Let me check with her. We were just about ready to have lunch," I confessed.

"Lunch, huh?" Peter chuckled.

"Yeah, Peter. Lunch. I'll call you back in a few," I remarked.

"Don't rush on my account."

Leave it to Peter to think something was going on, other than what was really going on. Slipping my phone in my pocket, I headed back to the kitchen. Jules had finished with the sandwiches and was ready to place them on a plate. Taking mine from her hand, I took a big bite and moaned, "Mmm… this is the best sandwich ever."

"Glad you like it," she replied, taking a bite of her own.

Taking our sandwiches with us, we sat at the dining table and enjoyed our lunch. With the last bite down. I looked over to Juliette and said, "Peter want us to come down to the shop. Hawk and Isabelle just got in and he would love for you to meet him. That is, after we finish our lunch?" I snickered.

"What's so funny, Ash?" she asked.

"Oh, nothing. When I told Peter that we were having lunch, he assumed that we were having lunch."

By the look on Juliette's face, she had no idea what I was talking about, but when I winked at her, she caught on. She must have had an appetite for something more than a ham sandwich, not that I would object. Standing to her feet, she walked over to where I was sitting and straddled my body, sending my cock to a full erection. Her lips sweetly caressed mine, teasing me before she nudged them open with her tongue. Forget about lunch, I was ready for dessert. Grabbing the globes of her tight ass, I stood up and carried her bear-style over to the couch. Before I put her down, her t-shirt was off, exposing the lacy see-through bra. Her bra should have been illegal the way it showed off her pert pink nipples. Lowering the cup of her bra, I began caressing the taut peak by rolling it between my fingers. A small whimper escaped her mouth, which sent a surge of desire to the tip of my cock.

Flipping her over, I slowly pulled off her shorts as I admired the firmness of her tight little ass. Running my hands down the soft skin of her legs, I dropped my head and kissed each cheek of her ass. Her back began to arch, lifting her gorgeous butt even higher in the air. Removing my own clothes, I adjusted my position and pressed my hard cock against her center. She was already wet for me, giving me the sleekness I needed to slip inside. Looking down at her creamy ass, my cock began to throb as I watched her sweet honey coat my shaft. Leaning over her body. I pulled her hair back and nibbled lightly on her ear and said, "Do you know how sexy you look right now with my cock pushing deep inside you?"

The only response was the moan of pleasure that escaped her mouth as her tongue brushed across her parted lips. Pushing her hips back to meet my thrusts, her body took every inch of me, squeezing my rod and taking every drop of desire from me. Reaching around her body, I placed my finger on her swollen clit, moving it in a circular motion until I could feel the crescendo of her own release take over. When our bodies finally relaxed, I lifted Juliette from the couch and headed to the bathroom for a quick shower, only we never made it there, nor did we make it to the shop to see Hawk and Isabelle.

CHAPTER TWENTY

Juliette

It felt wonderful to spend the day doing nothing but snuggling up against Ash. I did feel bad that we didn't go to the shop to visit with his dear friend Hawk and his wife Isabelle. If Hawk was like any of the other guys at Jagged Edge, I was pretty sure that he would be just as gorgeous as they were.

Gazing over to where Ash was lying, I turned my body and said, "If we are going to spend the whole day in bed, then someone is going to have to get some food."

With a beautiful smile, he looked over to me and said, "On it, babe," before he kissed me on the lips and slipped out from under the covers.

Laying back down on the fluffy pillow, I gawked at his ass as he headed to the bedroom door. It had to be the finest in New Jersey. Missing the closeness of his body, I pushed from the bed and grabbed a t-shirt from one of his drawers. It was too lonely in the room without him, and I was pretty sure he wouldn't mind a little company.

When I reached the kitchen, Ash wasn't there. I wasn't sure where he would have gone. He couldn't have gone too far, considering he had no clothes on. Walking over to the large windows in the living room, I looked out to find that he was leaning against the railing of the deck. I was thankful to see that he at least had a pair of jeans on.

Opening the door, I wandered over to where he was standing and stood beside him. I wasn't sure what he was looking at, but I could see that he was deep in thought. Placing my hand on his shoulder, I asked, "What's going on, Ash?"

As he looked over to me, my heart sank to my stomach, giving me the feeling that something bad had happened. Turning to face me, he took me in my arms and held me tight. "Peter wants to initiate the plan tomorrow. He got word that Sebastian and Walter were going to be leaving the States."

"There's something more. What aren't you telling me, Ash?" I asked calmly.

"I told Peter he needed to find another way to get to Sebastian. I can't risk losing you." Ash kissed the top of my head, which did nothing to tame the anger that was building up inside. As dangerous as this could be, there was no way that I could allow him to make that decision for me.

Fuming with fury. I pushed him away and vented my opinion. "It isn't your choice to make, Ash. I already told Peter that I would do whatever needed to be done to make sure those assholes never see the light of day again. I have to do this, Ash, with or without your permission."

"If you do this, Juliette, I am not going to watch something bad happen to you."

"Then don't."

I had never been so angry at one man before in my life. Hurrying to the door, I headed inside to pack my things and leave. I knew nothing was going to change Ash's mind and I couldn't be around a man who didn't understand me.

This was not about what he wanted, this was about what I needed to do so I could finally put this thing behind me.

Pulling my bag from the closet, I began throwing my things inside. All I wanted to do was get away from here. I wasn't even sure where I was going to go, but anywhere was better than here. Throwing my bag over my shoulder, I went to the front door and left. I could feel Ash's eyes on me, but he did nothing to stop me and there was no way I was going to turn around to see his expression. Sebastian and Mr. Marlow might have broken me, but Ash pretty much destroyed me.

~****~

Checking into a cheap motel, I pulled myself together and made a list of all the things I needed to take care of, the first being getting a new cell phone. Unpacking my things, since I knew I was going to be here for a while, I neatly stowed my bag in the closet before heading out.

Calling a cab from the motel phone, I waited in the rundown lobby until it arrived. The minute it pulled up, I told the driver to take me to the nearest wireless phone store. On the ride to the store, all I could think about was how much I already missed Ash. The worst part of it was that he didn't even come after me to tell me he was wrong. Wiping a tear from my eye, I decided I was not going to let what happened to us get me down. When he realized that he was wrong, I knew the he would contact me.

An hour later, I had a new cell in my hand. The first call I made was to the shop where my car was. Searching the Internet on my phone, I entered the name of the shop and pressed the call icon to be directly connected to them. When a man answered, I told him who I was and asked if my car was done. What surprised me the most was when I asked him how much the repairs were, he said they had already been taken care of.

The only person who would have done that was Ash. Just thinking about how great he was caused the tears to come rushing down. Raising my fingers to my mouth, I whistled as hard as I could to hail a cab. Before I had my hand away from my mouth, a yellow cab pulled up to the curb. I gave the driver the address to the shop and watched as he pulled away from the sidewalk

Thirty bucks later, I was driving my own car and headed back to the motel. By the time I arrived, the sun was already setting. I was emotionally exhausted from everything that had happened. Stretching out onto the bed, I kicked off my shoes and laid my head on the lumpy pillow. All I could think about was Ash and what he said. I knew that he didn't want me to get hurt, but he had to understand why I needed to do this. Sebastian had control over me for so long, I just wanted him to know what it actually felt like to be without control.

Reaching beside me, I grabbed my cell and searched for the number to Jagged Edge Security. The phone rang a couple of times before a strong, sexy voice answered, "Jagged Edge Security, Chavez speaking."

"Hi, Mike. It's Jules. Is Peter available?" I asked, taking a deep breath.

"Yeah, let me get him for you," he responded before placing me on hold.

Peter must have been preoccupied, because I was placed on hold for at least twenty minutes before he finally picked up and said, "Hewitt here."

"Hi, Peter. It's Jules," I replied before explaining my reason for calling. "Ash told me that you were going forward with the plan tomorrow."

"Yeah, he told me he talked to you," Peter confirmed hesitantly. "Listen, Juliette, maybe using you to find out where those girls are isn't such a good idea. We aren't even a hundred percent sure that Collins and Marlow are involved. I think it's better that we find another way."

I couldn't believe what I was hearing. There was no way I was going to give up. I knew that Sebastian and that slime ball were involved. "NO!" I shouted. "I have to do this, Peter. They can't get away with this. I know in my heart that they are involved. Who knows what they are going to do to all those girls? There isn't anyone else who knows those assholes as well as I do."

"Let me talk to Ash. If I can convince him that we will make sure nothing happens to you, maybe he will give in," Peter suggested.

"Thank you, Peter," I said, before I hung up the phone. I knew that if anyone could convince Ash that it would be okay, it was Peter.

Needing a shower, I scooted to the end of the bed and began undressing. Looking in the mirror, which was just outside the bathroom, my eyes looked swollen and tired. Turning on the faucet, I splashed some cold water on my face, hoping that would make me feel better. Even though my face looked better, my heart was another story. I didn't think there was anything that could fix it.

With a towel wrapped around my head and another around my body, I grabbed the complimentary lotion and began smoothing it on my skin. With every swipe of my hand across my skin, I kept remembering how it felt when Ash touched me. Laying back on the bed, I opened my towel to reveal my damp body. The cool air sent a tingle up my body, causing my nipples to become hard. Placing my hands on my breast, I closed my eyes and thought about Ash. Bringing my finger to my mouth, I sucked it just enough to coat it with my saliva. Using only the tip and slow circular movements, my nipple began to stand at attention, becoming sensitive to my touch.

I closed my eyes and pictured Ash in the room with me, even my voice reflected his presence as I commanded, "More, Ash, more."

Smoothing my other hand down my body, I felt the cool, damp skin beneath my touch. The feel of my bare mound sent a smile of satisfaction to my face, knowing that I kept it this way for Ash even though it was Sebastian who had requested it. My body began to quake, needing to be sated. Lowing my hand further, I separated my soft folds and began working one finger inside me. I could hear Ash's voice softly whisper, "God, you feel so good," as he continued his assault on my g-spot. Thrusting my hips upward, I needed to feel more of him inside me. Adding another finger to feel the fullness that his massive cock provided, I swayed my hips, increasing the friction that would send me over the edge. As my body jolted with pleasure, the tears fell.

~****~

When I got to the shop, Peter and another alpha-male type were having a conversation with Ash. It didn't surprise me that he would be there. I guess I just didn't want his eyes on me when I walked through the door. Stepping up to the three men, Ash lowered his head as though he was hiding his

238

expression. I knew that he still cared about me. It was evident by the way he looked at me when I came through the door.

"Hey," I said as I looked at Peter and avoided eye contact with Ash.

"Hey, Jules," Peter began before introducing me to the cute guy standing next to him. "Hawk, this is Juliette Daniels. She is the girl I was telling you about that is going to help us."

Before I could say anything, I heard a muffled remark from Ash, "So you think."

Ignoring his comment, I held out my hand and replied, "It's nice to meet you."

Breaking up our little group, Peter began walking towards the conference room. We all stood there for a minute before we finally figured out that he wanted us to follow him. Just as I was about to enter the conference room, Ash grabbed my arm and pulled me aside.

Dropping my eyes to where his hand gently gripped my arm, I bit my lip and said, "I need to do this."

239

Not expecting a kind word, Ash lowered his head and lightly kissed me on the lips and said, "I know."

There was a despondent look in his eyes, which I didn't know exactly how to decipher. I wasn't sure if it was because he knew he was beaten or because he was sorry. Placing my hand on his cheek, I asked, "Are you good with this?"

"Yeah, I'm good," he replied as he placed another soft kiss on my lips.

CHAPTER TWENTY-ONE

Ash

As soon as Juliette walked through the door, I knew that I had acted like an ass. I wanted so badly to go after her when she left yesterday, but my feet wouldn't move. My stubbornness took over and there was no way I was going to see the woman I love be put in danger. I thought the best way to take care if it was to let her go and get her out of my mind. One day without her was all I needed to realize that there was no way I would ever be able to let her go. And when I kissed her lips, that was all the confirmation I needed.

Taking my place next to her, I let her know that everything was good between us. Placing my hand on her thigh, I squeezed it lightly. Just the feel of her skin beneath my hand sent a surge to my groin. As soon as this meeting was over, I was going to satisfy the erection I got the minute I saw her.

"Okay, let's go over this so we can get out of here and get this job done," Peter's voice rang in the background, pulling me from my thoughts.

Peter was precise and detailed as he explained to everyone what their jobs would be. I had to admit, if everything went as smooth as Peter expected it to be, Sebastian Collins and Walter Marlow would be in custody before nightfall. Juliette didn't have to worry about her part. All she had to do was show up at Sebastian's office and let him know what happened to her. If he wasn't part of this, he would be reporting Walter Marlow to the authorities. If he was, then it would be a whole different scenario, which would involve the other guys. No matter what the outcome, Juliette would be covered. The only time she would be alone would be in his office, and even then she would be wired so we would know exactly what was going on. The minute it sounded like she was in trouble, we would get her out of there in a heartbeat.

Juliette and I left the shop in my truck so that we could get her suitable clothes for her meeting with Sebastian. I thought she looked gorgeous the way she was. Closing the door, she pulled her seat belt over her soft breast and asked, "So where are we going?"

Putting the truck in reverse, I gave her a quick look and said, "Fifth Avenue."

"Are you crazy, Ash? Do you know how expensive the shops are there?" Juliette advised.

"Of course, I do. Peter wanted to make sure you looked good. Even suggested you have a little makeover, not that you need one."

I could see Juliette rolling her eyes at me. Even though I had only ever seen her in cutsie shorts and jeans, I would have loved to see what she looked like all made up. My guess would be like a model on the cover of one of those girly magazines.

When we got to Fifth Avenue, I spotted a parking space and pulled right in. Opening the door, I fed the meter and waited for Juliette to get out. Looking up and down the street, I said to her, "Okay, where to first? Valentino's, New York & Company, Saks? Your choice."

"All of these places are too expensive," she argued.

Taking her by the hand, I had no other option but to decide for her. Walking up to a small boutique, I opened the door and gestured for her to enter. Her eyes rolled again at me as she walked passed me. With no reason other than having the urge, I smacked her on the ass and watched as her body jumped. I let out a little chuckle until her fist landed on my arm. I had to admit, for a small woman, she sure did have a mean punch.

While we were looking around the boutique, an older lady who looked to be in her forties walked up to us and asked in a polite but snobby way, "Is there something I can help you with?"

Juliette looked over to the woman and replied, "Nope, we're good."

The woman must have thought we were only looky-loos and wandered off back in the direction she came. Juliette grabbed a couple of dresses that she thought would work and headed to the dressing room. Sitting on a plush velvet chair in the waiting area just outside where the dressing rooms were, I waited, knowing that whatever she chose would look absolutely breathtaking on her.

When she stepped out of the dressing room, my jaw dropped to my chest. She was wearing a multicolored dress that fit snugly up against her breast and dipped low in the back, revealing the creamy softness of her back. Unable to hold back my amazement, I drooled, "Wow, Jules. You look amazing."

"I don't know if it is sexy enough," she professed.

"Jules, you are supposed to persuade Sebastian, not seduce him," I pointed out.

"Let me try on the next one?" she offered.

Slipping back into the dressing room, I was once again left waiting for her. Looking around the shop, I noticed that the shop clerk was looking my way. She tried to look away like she wasn't staring at me, but it didn't work. Moving away, she began busying herself on another rack of dresses. Juliette couldn't have appeared any quicker. I got the feeling from the evil stare that the old lady might have thought we were going to lift her dresses or something.

Every dress that Juliette tried on looked like it was made for her. She was gorgeous. She never considered herself that way so it didn't surprise me that she didn't take my compliment. Deciding to go with the first dress she tried on, we headed over to the register and placed it on the counter. Eighteen hundred dollars later, we were out of the shop and back in the truck with a beautiful dress, matching heels, and a necklace. Our next stop was the salon.

Arriving at the house, Juliette grabbed her purchased items and headed into the house. I knew that she was in a bit of a hurry considering we had spent more time at the shop than what we anticipated. Opening the door to the kitchen, she looked back over to me and said, "I'm going to take a quick shower."

Trying to be funny, I smiled and said, "Need any help with that?"

Flicking the cardboard lid to her expensive shoes, she managed to hit me in the head before she replied, "Very funny, Ash."

God, I love that woman, I thought as I watched her leave the kitchen. Her sassy little ass swayed back and forth like she knew I was watching her, which I was. Rocking back on my feet, I turned and went to the fridge to get a cold one.

246

Popping the top, I took a long draw and took the half-empty bottle with me to the living room. Standing by the window, I admired the orange-purple color that the sky held as the sun began to set. As beautiful as it was, it was also a signal that soon Juliette would be in the hands of Sebastian Collins. The only thing that I could think about was all the things that could go wrong. Concerned about the mission, I began asking myself all of the what-ifs. *What if Sebastian found the wire? What if he didn't go for her story? What if Walter Marlow was there when she arrived?* There were so many things that hadn't been taken into account. I knew that I was probably overthinking things, but I needed to make sure that Juliette remained safe.

Taking my cell from my back pocket, I dialed Peter. The second he answered I asked, "What if Sebastian finds the wire?"

I could hear Peter take a deep breath. "Ash, he won't."

"What if he doesn't buy her story?" I asked.

"He will, Ash. What is this really about, Ash? We have been over this already. Juliette knows what to do if things start to get heated," Peter assured me.

"I'm just really worried about her," I confessed. "I have a bad feeling about this."

Once again Peter told me not to worry. At first it was decided that I would stay clear of the mission because of my feelings for Juliette, but when Peter offered to let me go and to stay in the van that would be monitoring all of the activity, there was no way that I was going to say no. I might not be able to be right there with Juliette when she talked to Sebastian, but at least I would hear everything and be there in case we had to make a move.

Drinking the rest of my beer, I headed to the bedroom to check on Juliette. When I got there, she was in the bathroom touching up her make-up. I could have stood in the doorway and watched her all night. I watched as she picked up her lipstick and glided it on. God, how I wished I was gliding across her plump lips. Just the thought had my cock hard, wanting to plunge it deep inside her mouth and watch the pink gloss coat my throbbing member.

While I was lost in my lustful thoughts, she cleared her voice and lowered her eyes to my groin area. The reflection of her smile in the mirror told me that she was well aware of what was going on inside my jeans.

Fixing her lips by smacking them together, she said in a sexy voice, "You know, I could take care of that for you."

As much as I wanted her to, I knew that I wanted more than just a quickie. I wanted to take my time with her and worship every inch of her gorgeous body. Once again, I was lost in thought. Juliette walked to where I was standing and lightly placed her hand on my cheek. "It's almost time."

"I suppose there isn't any chance that you would consider changing your mind?" I inquired.

"I can't, Ash. I have to do this. Peter and you will make sure that nothing happens to me," she answered softly.

I would move the earth to make sure nothing happened to her. If Sebastian or Walter so much as hurt one hair on her pretty head, they could start digging their own graves.

CHAPTER TWENTY-TWO
Juliette

My nerves were all over the place as I got inside the fancy car that Peter rented for this mission. I had to admit that Lou looked pretty good in his chauffeur's getup. Ash convinced Peter to allow him to ride with me until we got closer to the Collins Building, while Peter, Ryan, Cop, Sly, and Hawk followed us in the van that was equipped with the surveillance equipment. Mike and Josh were already working on tapping into the security system by posing as security guards.

On the way to Sebastian's, Ash was holding my hand so tight that I could feel my blood supply being cut off. Placing my hand over his, I said softly, "Ash, babe, you have to loosen your grip."

"Sorry, Jules," he apologized, giving me a look that could have melted butter on a cold day.

I knew he was worried and didn't want me to get out of the car. If he had his way, he would tell Lou to just keep going, but I knew as much as his heart was with me, his common sense was with all those girls being held against their will.

We were a couple of blocks away from the Collins Building. Lou pulled over while the van pulled up beside him. What was supposed to be a quick exchange ended up being longer than expected. Ash, with his gorgeous eyes, looked at me with concern. "You be careful in there, Jules. If something doesn't seem right, you know what to do."

"I got this, Ash. All I have to say is 'The stars look beautiful,' and you guys will show up," I reiterated.

Hawk hit the horn, letting Ash know that it was time to go. Giving me a quick kiss, he opened the door and got out. My breath began to hitch as I watched him get into the van. Squeezing my eyes shut, I said in a soft voice, "You can do this, Jules."

The van pulled ahead and Lou eased away from the curb. Hawk took the next right, while Lou continued driving straight ahead. The closer he got to the building the tighter

251

my chest felt. Seeing the building through the window, Lou slowly pulled to the side. He looked over his shoulder and asked, "This is it. Are you ready?"

"I am," I answered, wondering if I would be able to pull this off. What could be so hard? All I had to do was convince Sebastian that I had made a mistake and let him know how I felt about him.

Opening the door, I stepped out of the car with my expensive Johnny Choo stilettos. The sidewalk wasn't as congested as the the early mornings were. Slowly, but confidently, I opened the door to the building and went inside. I was thankful to see that Josh and Mike were sitting behind the security desk. They both looked up to me in unison and then redirected their focus back to the monitors sitting in front of them.

I was only a few feet from where the elevators were, but it seemed like I walked up to them in slow motion. Even as I pressed the 'up' bottom, my finger lingered on the arrow pointing upward a little longer than needed. The doors soon opened and two gentlemen got off. I just stood there unable to move my feet. It was only when the doors began to close that I realized I needed to get into the car. Pushing the door open with my hand so that it would retract, I got in and turned my attention to the elevator panel and pressed the thirty-fifth floor. I took in another deep breath as the doors began to close.

Reaching the thirty-fifth floor, I was surprised to see that the bimbo with the fake boobs wasn't sitting behind the reception desk. Instead, it was a brunette wearing glasses looking like she just walked off the geek train. This was so very unusual, especially for Sebastian, considering he preferred the sexy stupid type. Walking up to her, I asked with confusion, "Where is Big-boo... I mean the other receptionist?"

The young receptionist lowered her glasses and looked up at me with a smile. "Sorry, who?" she asked, seeming like she had no idea what I was talking about.

"Never mind," I replied.

As I took a closer look at her, I realized that if it hadn't been for her glasses and the way her hair was pulled back, she would actually be quite attractive. Adjusting my stance, I placed my finger on my bottom lip to make sure that my lipstick wasn't where it shouldn't have been and continued with my performance. "Is Mr. Collins in?"

"He's in with a last minute appointment. If you would like to wait, I will let him know that you are here."

All I could think about at that moment was who could be his last minute appointment as I turned to take a seat on the leather chair in the reception area. Sitting there, I couldn't take my eyes off of the door at the end of the hall. If Mr. Marlow walked out of that door, I needed to make sure I had a quick escape.

I was just about to switch seats when I heard the voices of two men chatting. One I recognized as Sebastian's, but the other one I had never heard before. As Sebastian walked closer with the unknown gentleman, his eyes fell upon me with a look of surprise. I was pretty sure I was the last person he expected to see. Standing to my feet, I headed their way and said sternly, "We need to talk." I didn't know if it was the way he was looking at me or the fact that I looked pretty damn good that gave me my added confidence.

"We will talk tomorrow, Marcus," Sebastian stated as he shook the gentleman's hand.

254

When the elevator closed, Sebastian took me by the arm and began leading me towards his office. Giving his receptionist a rigid command, "No interruptions," he led me down the hall to his office. He had barely closed the door when he asked, "What are you doing here, Juliette?"

"I can't go back to him Sebastian, I just can't," I pleaded.

"You have no choice. A deal is a deal."

I watched as Sebastian walked over to the mini bar and poured himself a drink. This was it, the moment of truth. I knew the next words out of my mouth needed to be very convincing. Walking over to where he was standing, I placed my hand on his shoulder to make sure I gained his full attention. When his eyes met mine, I laid it on. "I can't go back to him, Sebastian, I love you." As hard as it was for me to say those words, I was pretty sure that he believed me.

Turning to face me, he pulled my body close to his and pressed his lips to mine. Parting my lips, I allowed him entrance into my warmth, trying desperately to think of something else other than his lips touching mine. His hands began slowly running down my bare back until he found my zipper. As he slid it down, I squeezed my eyes shut, knowing that if I stopped him from doing what he wanted to me, he would know that the declaration of my love was a lie.

While I was feeling that I had no other choice but to give in to him, the beep of his intercom sounded, saving me from my misery. A deep male voice came across the speaker, "Sir, this is security. There's an issue in the lobby that needs your immediate attention."

"Can't you handle it yourself?" Sebastian replied harshly.

"I'm sorry, sir, but he insists on your presence."

The call couldn't have come at a better time. When I got the chance, I needed to give Mike a big hug for stopping what might have just happened. Sebastian pulled the zipper back up on my dress and took hold of my hand. His grip was tight, which exhibited the annoyance he had at being interrupted. With me in tow, he looked over to the young receptionist and said, "You are free to leave," as though she was nothing more than his servant.

When the elevator arrived at the lobby, it wasn't long until we were off and standing in front of Mike and Josh at the security desk. Before either one of them could say a word, Sebastian demanded of them, "What the hell is this about?"

Mike stood and said, "The gentleman left, but said you knew where to find him. He said his name was Walter Marlow."

"That's just wonderful. Get me my driver," Sebastian ordered.

Sebastian turned towards me and gave me a light kiss on the forehead. With my eyes facing the security desk, Mike gave me a quick wink, letting me know that the seed just got planted and Lou would be here shortly to take us to where Walter would be. Spotting the car, Sebastian took hold of my hand and led me to the front door.

Lou got out of the car and was ready to open the back door when Sebastian asked, "Where is my usual driver, Max?"

"Sorry, Mr. Collins, he had a family emergency and was called away suddenly," Lou answered in a serious but convincing voice.

Lou was so convincing that even I believed his story. Tipping his head, he closed the door and rounded the sleek car and took his place behind the wheel. Looking in the review mirror, he asked, "Where to, Sir?"

"Just drive, I'll tell you when to turn," Sebastian barked.

This is not the response that Lou was looking for. What he really needed was a physical address so that the guys on the other end of the wire would know where we were going. I only hoped that they would be able to figure out the direction that we were heading by Sebastian's instructions.

Leaning my head against his shoulder to gain his trust, I asked softly, "Where are we going, Sebastian?"

"To end this deal with Walter," he professed.

His answer didn't do anything to help out the guys. I needed to use a different approach if I was going to get a

258

location out of him. Snuggling closer, trying not to lose my lunch, I spoke softly when I asked, "Are we going to the rundown mansion on Graypeak Drive?"

"It's the only place where he would be, pet," he answered with a sympathetic look that I had never witnessed before.

Just as I looked forward, I saw Lou look at me in the review mirror, giving me a smile. I knew then that the guys had a location as to where we were going.

~****~

When Lou turned down Graypeak Drive, my body began to tense. Just the thought of being near that man again made my skin crawl with disgust. How could I ever look at him after everything he had done to me, to my home, to my life? Stopping in the circular drive in front of the entrance, Sebastian opened the door and got out before Lou was able to assist him. When he held out his hand, I placed mine inside his and allowed him to help me out of the car. Lou remained in the car as Sebastian and I walked up to the front door. It didn't surprise me that he didn't knock, announcing our presence; he did, after all, own the house.

Walking through the door, the same musty smell hit my senses and just about knocked me over. It must have affected Sebastian the same way as he held his hand to his nose. As he advanced further inside, I followed close behind him, using him as some sort of shield against what was to come. The closer we got to a set of double doors the stronger the scent of cigar smoke became. Sliding the doors open, there, standing near the large window, was Walter Marlow. Without so much as a look in our direction, he spoke in a gruff voice, "I see you found her, yet I don't understand how she escaped the fire."

Sebastian walked closer to where he was standing and questioned him about his comment. "What are you talking about, Marlow?"

Turning our way to address Sebastian's question, his eyes were drawn to me. "She should have died in that fire. The minute I got the call from my loyal servant, I knew exactly where she would be going. With a little incentive, my men were able to beat her there and make sure she was tucked securely inside. I guess I underestimated your willingness to live. Although, I don't believe you got out on your own."

"You bastard," I yelled, staying where I stood. "You boarded my house."

With an arrogant chuckle, he confirmed what I already knew. "Not me, Slave. Call it a service well paid for."

Holding back his own anger, Sebastian seethed, "That wasn't part of the deal, Marlow."

"Yeah, well, neither was her getting away. I couldn't risk her telling everyone what she saw," Marlow replied.

"I didn't see anything, you stupid troll of a man. I didn't have to. I know all about the girls. You both disgust me."

I was so angry that I didn't realize what I was saying until it was too late. Sebastian had his hand on my arm gripping it so tightly, I thought that he was going to rip it from my body. "You little cunt," he growled. "You played me, but what I don't understand is why."

Ripping the dress from my body, he took hold of it and began searching the material. When he didn't find what he was looking for, he took hold of my necklace and twisted it around my neck, causing my airway to be constricted. With his teeth clenched together, he asked, "Where the fuck is it?"

Unable to breath, I pointed to the barrette in my hair; it was where Peter had planted the microphone, which was no larger than the tip of a pencil eraser. Sebastian pulled it from my hair, taking several strands with it, and threw it to the floor, where he placed his heel over it and crushed it.

This was not how it was supposed to be. Even though I gave myself away, the guys should have been here already. I couldn't let Sebastian know that I was affected by this. Even when his hand landed across my face, I knew I needed to remain strong.

Still half dazed, I heard Walter talking to someone on the phone. The only words I managed to hear were 'girls and away' before he hung up the receiver. Moments later, a large man who looked like he hadn't taken a shower in months appeared at the door. Walter walked up to me and placed his hand on my cheek, the same one that Sebastian had slapped minutes before. "You shouldn't have run away," he said before looking at the large man. "Put her with the others and get the van ready."

The large man slung me over his shoulder like I was nothing. I had never felt more humiliated in my life. The way he looked at my bare breasts, I thought for sure that he was going to eat me alive. And now to have him take me away, who knew what he was going to do?

CHAPTER TWENTY-THREE

Ash

I knew the minute her hidden microphone went dead that something went wrong. We were still ten minutes out and running out of time. Hawk laid on the gas, but with the traffic, he could only do so much to hurry. There was one upside to this mess: Lou was there letting us know what was going on. Even though he couldn't get close enough without being seen, at least he would be able to tell us if anyone left.

Trying hard to keep my composure, I looked to Peter for some answers. "So, what now?"

"We will need to stick to the plan. We were ready for this. Not every plan is going to be one hundred percent on target. There are going to be some bumps along the way. That is why there is always a back-up plan," Peter assured me as he pulled his cell from his pocket.

"Lou. Hewitt. Do you have eyes on Juliette?" Peter asked in a commanding voice, putting Lou on speaker so I and the rest of the guys could hear.

"That's a negative, Peter. There's no way to look inside the house from here and besides, all the curtains are drawn. Unless you want me to knock on the door and ask, there is no way to know what is going on inside," Lou responded.

"Is there a way you can get inside without being noticed?" I asked. The only way Lou was going to make sure that Juliette was okay was to get inside the house.

"Give me a minute," Lou advised as the phone line went silent.

I had never felt so helpless. If I thought jumping out of the van and running to where Juliette was would help, I would have done it in a heartbeat. My patience was slowly beginning to dwindle and was being replaced by tension.

All of us were sitting in the van waiting in anticipation for Lou to get back on the line. Hawk was driving like a madman and getting the finger from everyone that he cut off. With a crackle of the speaker, Lou finally came back on.

"I wasn't able to see anything, guys. There wasn't even a crack between the curtains that I could peek through," Lou reported. "Our only option is for me to go inside."

"Negative, Lou. We should be there in five. Keep us posted if you see any movement," Peter ordered.

Peter was right. The last thing that we needed was for Lou to get caught inside the house. Before Peter could hang up, Lou exclaimed, "Peter, a van just pulled out front. Something is going down."

"Sit tight, Lou, we are almost there," Peter ordered.

"You got it, boss, but you better hurry."

With the new information Lou had just shared with us, we knew that our window of opportunity was closing. There was only one reason a van would be at the mansion: it was to transport the women, and that meant Juliette too. Stepping on the gas, we were just out of Manhattan when the worst thing possible happened. The road that we needed to take was blocked by a three car pile up. We knew that it was going to be hours before this mess would be cleaned up. Hawk looked in the side mirror hoping that he could back out of the mess, but even that was a no-go. There were cars stopped behind us at least two blocks deep. Making my way to the front of the van, I looked through the windshield to see if I could find a way out of here. Scanning our surroundings, it was then that I noticed an officer speaking to the driver of an SUV at the front of the line closest to the accident. If we could get the police officer to divert the traffic around the block, then we could get past the accident and be on our way.

Opening the door to the van, I jumped out and headed toward the officer. Running between the cars, I finally made it to where the officer was still chatting with the driver. Leave it to a beautiful woman to distract him. It wasn't that I blamed him, it was that I needed his attention. Tapping him on the shoulder since he obviously didn't see me standing next to him, I motioned him away from the gorgeous driver.

"We need your assistance. My name is Ash Jacobs and I work for an elite security company known as Jagged Edge," I began, pulling my ID from my pocket. "If you could divert this traffic around the block, we could get by."

The officer looked at me like I was feeding him a bunch of shit, giving me one of those 'Fuck off' looks. "Look... Mr. Jacobs of Jagged Edge Security..." he mocked as he lifted my ID to look at the name. "I don't give a rat's ass who you work for, this traffic isn't going anywhere until this accident is cleared up."

I could feel my body begin to tighten at his arrogance. I was so close to popping him one. If it wasn't for Peter coming up behind me, I would have done just that. Holding me back, Peter looked to the officer and confirmed what I tried to tell him. "Officer Benson," Peter began as he looked to his name badge. "Just like you, we are trying to do our jobs. Saving lives is our number one priority, as I'm sure it is yours as well. All we are asking is that you divert the traffic around the block. Besides, with the cars out of the way, the paramedics would have better access in getting to the victims and out of here quickly."

I didn't know what it was about Peter, but he always managed to talk people into doing things they wouldn't normally do. By the time we got back to the van, the traffic was diverted and we were on our way. This was a setback that we didn't need. Not only were we now taking a detour, it just added an additional ten minutes to reach to the mansion.

Hawk took every shortcut that he could think of to get us there quicker, but even then, it only delayed our arrival more. It seemed like no matter how hard we tried, this mission was beginning to look like it was jinxed.

When we were finally able to get to the main road that would take us to the mansion, Peter's cell rang. It was Lou. All of us took a deep breath, hoping it wasn't the news that we were too late.

"What do you have for me, Lou?" Peter asked reluctantly.

"The girls were just loaded into the van and they are getting ready to head out. Need to know your ETA," Lou admitted.

"We are less than five minutes away," Peter confirmed.

"Well, you better make it two, because the driver and his buddy just got in the van," Lou stated.

"Shit, can you detain them?" Peter asked.

"I'll do what I can," Lou replied.

With only two minutes to get there, Hawk laid on the gas and the van took off like there was a turbo boost behind his foot.

Reaching the house, we barely made it in time to see the van turn from the main drive onto the road we were currently on. With a quick turn of the wheel, Hawk made a one-eighty, managing to keep the van on the road without driving into the ditch. Keeping our distance, we followed them for about ten miles until they made a turn to the left and pulled up to an old empty warehouse. There was no one else around as we slowed up and waited. The only reason for the stop would be to make an exchange for the girls. Losing my patience, I turned to Peter and asked, "What are we waiting for? Let's get the girls and get out of here."

"Don't you want this kind of thing to stop? If we don't let the exchange happen, we will never know who is behind this," Peter stated as he placed his hand on my shoulder, knowing just how I felt. "Look, Ash, I know how bad you want Juliette out of that van, but we have to wait, at least until they get here. Then we will move in."

I knew Peter was right. I wanted to get all the scumbags involved. As long as we got to them before the girls got out of the van, I knew she would be okay. Taking my place towards the front of the van, I watched and waited for someone to show up. About twenty minutes passed and there was still no sign of anyone. It was then that we figured out that we had been taken. Someone should have been here by now.

Pulling his cell from his pocket, Peter dialed Lou, who was still back at the house. "Lou, I think we got scammed. Is there any movement at the house?" Peter questioned, concerned that they may have made the wrong move.

"Nothing, Peter. Nobody has gone in or come out," Lou confessed.

Things just weren't making sense. It was then that Peter advised, "Guys, I think we've just been played. Hawk, you know what to do."

Hawk was in motion and within seconds he had the van angled sideways so that the other van had nowhere to go. Sliding the back door open, Peter jumped out with Sly, Cop,

271

and I close behind. Hawk and Ryan also exited the van. We were all armed and ready to fire when the driver and his sidekick opened their doors with their hands held high above their heads. It was like they had planned this whole thing. I kept my gun pointed at the driver, while Sly had his on the other guy.

Peter was already heading to the other side of the van to open the door. I could hear the door slide with a loud "Shit, motherfucker," comment coming from Peter. It was then that I knew they were either badly hurt or dead. Unable to hold back, I rounded the front of the van to see for myself. Peter had backed away from the van a few steps and was walking in circles while running his hand through his hair. I knew it was bad. Looking inside the van, there was nothing, it was empty. I didn't know if I was relieved or pissed off. I guess I was more pissed, because I took the guy that Sly was watching and threw him up against the side of the van.

With gritted teeth and fury, I demanded, "Where the fuck is she?" I couldn't wait for him to answer. The shit grin on his face was enough for me. With one blow to his face, his nose was broken and the blood started spilling.

"You broke my fucking nose," the man claimed.

Holding him by the collar, I looked straight into his eyes and asked again, "Where?"

When he saw my fist coming at him, he began to sing. "They are all still at the mansion. We were informed to just go, leave without them, and drive here."

We didn't have time for these losers, so Hawk grabbed a few long zip-ties and secured the men to the side mirrors, one on each side of the van. Once they were secure with no chance of escape, Peter made a quick call to the NYPD and let them know of the location.

When we began to drive off, the only thing I could think about was Juliette. I would never be able to forgive myself if anything happened to her, and I sure as shit could never forgive Peter.

CHAPTER TWENTY-FOUR
Juliette

After the beastly giant was ordered to get me something to cover myself, he ushered me down a sparsely lit staircase that led to the basement of the house. I could hear water dripping from somewhere, but I wasn't sure where. The floor was wet and the walls were moist and covered in a black moss-like substance. Unable to really see anything, my eyes finally focused and I couldn't believe what I saw. There were so many of them, and now I was among them.

I wasn't sure how long they had been down here, but they all backed away from the cell door and huddled into the nearest corner. My body jumped as Mr. Giant slammed the cell door shut. Moving closer to the women, I was able to get a better look at them. They all looked like they hadn't seen a shower for some time. It also looked like they weren't getting the nutrition they needed either.

Trying to get some answers, I spoke in a soft voice and asked, "How long have you been here?"

274

One of the girls from the back stepped up and said, "It's hard to say. Most of us haven't seen light for days, maybe even months."

The girl who spoke couldn't have been more than eighteen. Matter of fact, a lot of them looked to be very young. Maybe even younger than her. Stepping closer to the group of girls, I said quietly, "My name is Juliette."

The girls began to open up to me as they told me their names. Most of them were from Mexico, while the rest were from the States or brought here on a freight liner and held in a large cargo container. I couldn't even imagine what these girls went through. The longer we talked, the more they got to know me. I told them about the men at Jagged Edge and our plan to get them out of here, at least until they found my wire.

It turned out that most of them were taken in broad daylight. The girls that weren't were traded in exchange for debts that were impossible to repay. Each girl had a different story. There was even one girl, her name was Kimberly, who was a college student at UCLA working on her medical degree to become a pediatric doctor. She was taken right from the college campus when she was walking to the library. So many of them, each with a different story.

Walking over to the door, I examined the lock to see if maybe there was a way to work it open. As old as this house was, maybe the lock was old too, and I could somehow pry it open. I needed something to stick in the lock, but the way things looked there wasn't anything sharp enough to use. Even a hairpin would be better than nothing. That was when I noticed that one of the girls had her hair pulled back in a bun, which meant she would be using hairpins to keep it in place. Walking up to where she was sitting, I looked down on her and asked, "Do you have a hairpin?"

Reaching behind her head, she removed one of her hairpins and handed it to me. I knew that there wasn't much time before they would be coming back to get us. Manipulating the pin, I straightened it out enough that I could work both ends together to work the lock. When I heard voices, I knew I was too late, they were coming for us. Stepping away from the door, I needed to think of something fast before they showed up. Placing the hairpin in Kimberly's hand, I crouched over and began to moan like death had taken over my body. If I couldn't save myself, maybe I could at least save them.

When the men came into view, Mr. Giant was in front with another man following behind him. Looking over to me as he opened the door, he growled, "Get up, we're taking you lovely ladies to your new home."

When he grabbed me by the shirt, I looked at him and pleaded, "I can't move, I think I am going to be sick," as I continued to pull my body into a ball and moaned like I was in a lot of pain.

Mr. Giant must have believed me. His hands were around my body, carrying me out of the cell and back from where they came. I gave Kimberly a smile and hoped that she would have enough time to get out of the cell. I just hoped that I could keep my act up before they figured out that I was faking it.

When we got to the study, I was placed on the long sofa. Sebastian and Mr. Marlow weren't in the room, which I thought was very odd. Pushing myself to a sitting position, I tried to look out of the double doors that were left open when the two he-men left. I was pretty confident that neither Sebastian nor Mr. Marlow were around, so I stood from the couch and hurried over to the window. Pulling back the dark curtains, I looked out over the drive to see if I could spot Lou in the black car. The drive was too long for me to see anything. I knew that the best thing I could do would be to try and get out of here. I had this terrible feeling that being left alone was not just dumb luck. The two goons that took me here were probably standing just outside the door, waiting for me to make a move.

Settling back on the couch, I decided to take my chances. Continuing with my act, I laid my head against the back of the couch and waited for Sebastian and Mr. Marlow to show up. Thinking they were never going to show, I heard what sounded like a car engine that needed a new muffler outside. Curious to see what it was doing out there, I headed to the window once again and drew back the curtains. Pulled up close to the door was a black van. My heart sank into my stomach as I watched the girls being loaded inside. I needed to do something. I couldn't let this happen. Running to the doors leading out of the study, I was stopped abruptly by the smell of a man I would never forget. He was standing there with his goons, one either side of him like a pair of bookends.

I tried to get passed them, but my efforts were worthless as Mr. Giant picked me up like a sack of potatoes. Screaming and hitting him, I cursed, "Let go of me, asshole."

He didn't care. His only reaction was a low and annoying laugh. Mr. Marlow must not have found it very funny; his voice came out sharply as he said, "Enough."

The giant set me down, but still held onto my arms as Mr. Marlow placed his index finger under my chin so that I was looking directly into his evil eyes. "Why would you do that, my little pet? Do you enjoy being punished?"

I wasn't sure what I was thinking, but I spit in his face, only to receive a slap across the cheek. "You will never get away with this, sicko," I yelled as I tried once again to pull free.

"Take her upstairs and tie her to the bed face down," he began as the ogre began leading me out of the room. "Oh, and make sure she is completely naked. I don't want anything to get in the way for what I have planned for her."

I had no idea what he had planned for me, but there was no way in hell that he was ever going to lay a hand on me. I needed to figure out a way to get out of this.

~****~

Maybe I should have thought twice about acting like I was sick. If I hadn't been so stupid, I would be with the rest of the girls and not here. When Mr. Giant ripped my clothes off and tied me to the bed, he couldn't have been more rough. I had never been more humiliated in my life from the way he stuck his tongue out and licked the side of my face after he had me secured to the bed. He even went so far as to slap my ass before he left.

As bad as it was for me, I kept thinking about how bad it was for those girls. I kept wondering what would happen to them. They were on their way to who knew where. Pulling on my restraints, I tried to break free, but the harder I pulled, the tighter they got. It was useless. Somehow I had to block out what was going to happen once that slimeball got a hold of me. Resting my head against the rough pillow, I tried to think of something else. The only thing that made me happy was thinking about Ash. As my mind began to wander, I thought about how it would be if I never signed that stupid contract. Would I still be in college or would I be one of those high school girls who ended up marrying whomever she could just in order to make it in this world? But most of all, I wondered if my life would have included Ash. Would we have ever met?

CHAPTER TWENTY-FIVE

Ash

As we were heading back to the old mansion, I kept thinking about what we might find once we got there. The best scenario would be that the girls were still there and Juliette was safe. I had a funny feeling it was only wishful thinking on my part.

Even though Hawk was driving well over the speed limit, it was taking too long to get there. About the time that we got out of the city, Peter's cell began going off. Moving to where he was sitting, I could see that it was Lou calling as he swiped his finger across the screen.

"Lou, please tell me that you have something good for us," Peter hinted.

"Well, some bad and some good, I think," Lou replied.

"Hit me with it," Peter requested as he put the call on speaker. "I've got you on speaker so the guys can hear."

"Well, another van pulled up. Black this time. About a dozen girls got in. From what I could tell, none of them were Juliette, which means she is still in the house," Lou paused for a moment. "You might have your work cut out for you. They haven't left yet, but there is a guy sitting inside, waiting for the driver, I suspect. I'm not sure how many more may be inside."

Peter ran his hand through his short hair, contemplating what to do. The closest person to the mansion was Lou, and we were at least another ten to fifteen minutes out. Finally, he got back on the phone and said, "Here is the plan, Lou. When that van leaves, I want you to follow it. Call Mike and let him know exactly where you are. There is no reason for him and Josh to remain at the Collins Building. Let them know where you are. Hopefully they will be able to head off the van. Me and the other guys, I'm pretty confident, will be able to handle whomever is in the house. I will let our friends at the FBI know what is going on so they can assist you and help get those girls to safety. Be careful, Lou."

The minute Peter hung up the phone, I knew that his decision to order Lou to stay with the van was because of me. It was very unlikely that Sebastian and Marlow would be going anywhere real soon. Looking over to him, I patted him on the shoulder and said, "Thanks, bro."

With an understanding look, he yelled to Hawk from the back of the van, "Step on it, Hawk."

"You got it, boss," Hawk replied as he laid his foot on the gas.

~****~

The van must have taken off because Lou was nowhere in sight. To keep from being seen, Hawk parked the van down the road from where the drive to the rundown mansion was. As Peter went over the plan, all I wanted to do was to get to Juliette before it was too late. We had no idea what was in store for us once we got inside the house. I knew that having a plan was needed, but me getting to Juliette was the only plan I had.

Grabbing what we needed, we all slowly made our way to the old house. Aside from the dead trees that lined the drive, there wasn't much with regard to coverage for us. The last thing we needed was to be seen or be open targets. Maneuvering though the trees, we finally made it to the mansion. There was no way to look inside given that all of the curtains were drawn, and going through the front door was out, unless we wanted to get caught before we even got inside. Peter signaled for us to proceed to the back of the house. He, Sly, and I went around the left side, while Hawk and Cop went around to the right.

Meeting at the back of the house, there was no other entrance inside except the back door. Deciding on how to gain entrance, Peter thought it would be better for him to enter first. Working the lock, I managed to get it open. As I turned the knob and slowly pushed open the door, it began to creak a little louder than we liked. Ready to take on any unexpected complications, we raised out weapons.

When we stepped through the door, we stepped into a room that looked a mud room more than anything else. It also looked like maybe this entrance hadn't been used very much based on the clutter. Navigating through the mess, we came upon another door. Since Peter was in front, he slowly turned the handle and carefully pulled the door open. We all took a deep breath, hoping that this door was well oiled, allowing us entrance without giving off our location. As we walked through the door, the room we entered was the kitchen. Still, there was no sight of anyone around. Peter once again took the lead.

Reaching the swinging doors leading out of the kitchen, Peter took one side while I took the other. There was a round window at the top of the door, like you would see in an old restaurant. We rose to full height and looked for any signs of movement. Looking at each other, Peter whispered in a low voice, "There is no way this could be this simple."

Nodding my head, I replied, "This is a big house. I'm sure they are here somewhere, Peter."

Peter and I pushed open the door as we all stayed low, even as we passed the long dining table. Everything about this old mansion gave me the impression that Sebastian didn't want to waste any time on the upkeep. The carpeting was worn and the wood could have used a good oiling. Even though it seemed to be fairly clean, it was old and definitely run down. We made it to the open entry. It was then that we heard a familiar voice.

"There is no need to treat her like some animal, Walter," Sebastian's voice sounded with animosity.

"She is no longer your property, therefore, no longer your concern," Walter reminded him. "Now if you will excuse me, I need to do what I should have done a long time ago."

Holding our positions, we waited until Walter was out of the room before we closed in on Sebastian. Since we didn't hear any other voices, we were pretty sure that he was alone. With Peter's go-ahead, we followed his direction, with Hawk and Cop sent to check out the rest of the house. Peter instructed Sly to stay where he was while he and I headed in Sebastian's direction.

When we got to the room, Sebastian was facing the window with the curtain fully drawn, I could see that he had a drink in his hand. I thought for sure we entered the room without him knowing, but when he said, "I knew you would eventually show up," I found out I was wrong.

Unwilling to take any shit, I snarled, "Where the fuck is she?" as I began moving in on him.

"He has her upstairs, but you need to hurry. I think his plan is to kill her after he is finished with her," Sebastian confessed, not moving from his spot.

With my gun drawn, I grabbed him by his suit collar and hissed, "You are going to show us where, you piece of shit."

Shifting his body, we began moving out of the study and into the main entrance, where we began moving up the staircase. We met up with Sly, who followed us upstairs. Making our way down a long hallway, Sebastian stopped and pointed to a door. Handing him over to Peter, I held my gun high and slowly turned the doorknob. As Juliette came into view, I could see that she was tied to the bed, fully naked, with Marlow standing above her with a gun pointed at her head. Not thinking, I yelled, "Stop, you motherfucker."

His gaze switched to mine and a contorted look of disgust crossed his face. "Well, well. It seems you are a little too late, Casanova. Come any closer and she's dead."

"Don't do this, Marlow," I seethed.

"Then I suggest you back off."

287

There was no way that I could leave Juliette in the hands of this madman. I knew that If I had any chance to get her out of here safely, I needed to back down, or at least make him think I was going to. When I lowered my weapon, he began untying her. I watched his every move as he ordered, "Stand up, Slave, and for God's sake cover yourself.

My temperature was boiling as I gazed over at Juliette as she pushed from the bed and wrapped the sheet around her body. *"What the hell did he do to her?"* I thought to myself as my hand tightened around the grip of my gun. Her hair was matted and her face was tear soaked, with her makeup smeared on her cheeks and under her eyes. If that wasn't the worst, it was when she looked at me that I knew what he had done.

I wasn't sure what happened, but just as I was about to raise my gun to kill this asshole, my gun was taken from me. Everything began moving in slow motion as Sebastian shouldered me, knocking me to the floor. The sound of my gun being fired filled the room as I set my sights on Juliette. Her body hunched to the floor and her hands moved to cover her head. Marlow raised his gun and fired. It was like I could see the bullet move through the air before it landed against Sebastian's chest, sending him downward. Thinking of only protecting Juliette, I picked up my gun from where it had fallen to the floor and aimed it at Marlow. As I pulled the trigger, Marlow aimed his gun at Juliette. My heart began to race as I unloaded five more rounds.

Everything was no longer in slow motion. One of the bullets I shot off hit Marlow on the wrist, which sent his bullet upward. He was still standing, but not for long. His body began to crumble as I watched the blood ooze out of his head. When he hit the floor, I was up on my feet and by Juliette's side. Her body was still crouched in a fetal position as I wrapped my arms around her. All I care about was protecting her. Lifting her in my arms, I carried her over to the bed and held her on my lap as I cradled her in my arms. Rocking her like a small child, I whispered the only words I knew she would understand. "I love you, Juliette. I will never leave you again."

Her arm came around my shoulders and her head nuzzled in the crook of my neck. In a barely-there whisper, she said, "I love you too."

CHAPTER TWENTY-SIX
Juliette

Even though almost everything I owned got burned in the fire, Ash did everything he could to make his home mine too. It had been almost a month since Ash and the guys came to my rescue, and in the end, Sebastian Collins and Walter Marlow got what they deserved. I was glad to hear that Lou, Mike, and Josh were able to get to girls in time and prevent them from being taken out of the country. Who would have thought the man who kept me under his control for so long had been associated with the biggest human trafficking ring in North America? And to top it off, to have someone like Walter Marlow as his partner.

The hardest thing about this whole ordeal was telling my mom what had happened and what I had kept from her all these years. I thought for sure she would be angry with me, but instead she insisted on flying out here to see for herself that I was okay and that Ash was the right boy for me. I will never forget the look on her face when she finally met Ash. Calling him a boy was an understatement, she confessed after seeing him. Sometimes I think she wished she was twenty years younger.

Sitting on the deck soaking in the warmth of the sun in nothing more than a skimpy swimsuit and a t-shirt, I took a drink of my beer as I watched a handsome man walking up the steps towards me. God, he was perfect in so many ways. Sitting beside me, I handed him a beer that I had chilling in the cooler. Looking over to him, I gave him a smile and asked, "So what do you think, big guy?"

Taking a pull from his beer, he looked out in the distance and replied, "I think the next time your mom decides to come visit, we will put her up in a nice hotel. I couldn't even look at you without her giving me that look."

"What do you mean, 'that look'?" I questioned

"The look that mothers give a man when they think the man's intentions are less than honorable," Ash explained.

I had to laugh at him. For one thing, my mom would never give him that kind of look, and for another, I saw the look she was giving him. It was a look of envy, not concern over his intentions with me. Standing to my feet, I bent over

291

and kissed Ash on the lips before voicing my opinion. "You're wrong, Mr. Jacobs. That look she was giving you was her approval, and maybe a little bit of jealousy that she isn't younger."

Before I could take another step, Ash pulled me to his level, causing my body to land on his lap. His lips fell upon mine and in a heated breath, he said, "I think we should test that theory."

Without any effort, Ash had me in his arms and he carried me through the double doors. His lips were on mine and I couldn't get enough of him. Making it to the bedroom, he gently placed me on the bed. He moved his hand under my t-shirt and gently began caressing my breasts through the thin material of my swim top. His touch sent electric currents through my body. Lowering his head, Ash began trailing soft kisses up my body. Easing the cup of my swimsuit aside, he caressed the swollen tips of my nipples with his tongue, while his hand slid down across my belly. Lifting his head from my pert nipple, his lips met mine and my arms wrapped around him to bring him closer. As our kiss deepened, he began lowering my bottoms down my legs. His finger dipped inside my channel, searching for the one spot that would send me soaring.

Breaking our kiss, he showered kisses along my jaw, down my neck, and over my shoulder. With his free hand, he pulled the string to my top and pulled it away, leaving my body ready to be adored. Once again, his mouth was on my sensitized bud, lapping and sucking it to a hard peak. I could feel my back lift from the bed as the sensations from all sides began to take over. Reeling in the feel of his touch, my body was begging for more. When his mouth lowered to my mound, I lost all control. My body began to pulsate as his tongue swirled lightly around my clit. When he inserted another finger inside me, my body unleashed, pouring out the pleasure inside. Slowly moving up my body, Ash placed his mouth over mine and dipped his tongue inside. Just the taste of my essence on his tongue had me undone. Before I could tell him "More" his jeans were off and his hard cock was inside me, giving me more of what I wanted. The air around me seemed to electrify, answering the rapid thud of my heart as he pushed deeper inside me. Unable to hold on any longer, I could feel my walls tighten around his thick girth and I soon let go, feeding his thirst.

Maybe it was everything that had happened over the past month or maybe it was the fact that I was finally in charge of my own destiny, but the emotions began to spill from my eyes. Holding on to Ash as tight as I could, my mind felt like, for the first time, it was alive. Jumping from the bed and out of his arms, I decided I wanted to do something crazy. Standing before him in all my naked glory, I put my hands on my hips and commanded, "Get out of bed, we are going to walk down to that little pond and go skinny dipping."

I could tell by the look on his face, he wasn't too keen about my suggestion. Holding out my hand, I snapped my fingers, letting him know that I was serious about this. Finally, after contemplating whether or not I needed to be institutionalized, Ash placed his hand in mine and rose from the bed. Smiling at me as he put his jeans on, he took my naked body in his arms and said, "I think that I have fallen in love with a crazy woman."

Slapping him on the shoulder, I replied, "Come on. It will be fun."

Slipping on my t-shirt and only the bottoms to my swimsuit, I grabbed a couple of towels from the bathroom and slipped on my sandals. Ash was already down in the kitchen packing a small cooler with only a couple of beers inside. Heading out the door, we began walking down the narrow path that would take us to the small pond. While I wished that I had chosen a different pair of shoes, Ash could tell I was having problems walking on the uneven ground. Stopping in his tracks, he turned his back towards me and said, "Hop on."

Taking a good leap, I jumped up onto his back and hugged his bear-style. The heat of the sun was heating our bodies and the thought of cooling off in the pond was sounding better and better. When we reached the pond, there wasn't a soul in sight. Taking the initiative, I stripped off my clothes first, very slowly, giving Ash a provocative strip show. Before I could get to the water, Ash had me up and in his arms with his lips pressed to mine. Everything about this moment was perfect. If I hadn't suggested it, I would have thought that Ash had planned this last-minute rendezvous himself. Placing me back on my feet, he broke our kiss and placed his hand on my cheek. There was something different about the way he looked at me.

Concerned that something might be wrong. I put my hand over his and asked, "What is it, Ash? What's wrong?"

Taking both of my hands in his, he lowered his head for a brief moment as if he was thinking about what to say. When he lifted his head, I knew then what this was about. I

295

knew it was over and this was his way of breaking up with me. My heart began to beat faster and my breath began to hitch. It wasn't what I thought at all as he lowered to his knee. His voice was soft as he said, "Juliette…"

Before he could usher another word, I shouted excitedly, "Wait… not another word, Ash. You are not going to do what I think you are going to do with me standing here naked."

Grabbing my clothes, I hurried and put them on, even knowing that my t-shirt was inside-out. Standing before him, I took both his hands and said, "Okay, go ahead."

Ask began to chuckle at me, causing him to have a difficult time saying what needed to be said. With an annoyed look, I scolded him, "Ash, this is not funny."

Switching his position to his other knee, he once again looked up to me. This time I didn't stop him. "Juliette, I know that we haven't known each other for very long, but I have never loved a woman as much as I love you. I want to spend the rest of my life with you. I want to share everything with you. Will you stay with me forever as my wife?"

I thought I would stop breathing when he said those words. Falling to his level, I placed my hand on his cheek and said the only thing I could, "Hell, yeah," before placing my lips to his.

It was like nothing else mattered as our lips found each other's. This was my true destiny and no one was ever going to take it away from me again. I couldn't image spending my life without him. He had shown me that there really is love in the world and two people could actually find each other to share it with. Everyone deserved to be loved, including me.

About the Author

Some would call me a little naughty but I see myself as a writer of spicy thoughts. Being an erotic romance writer is something that I never imagined I would be doing. There is nothing more rewarding than to put your thoughts down and share them. I began writing three years ago and have enjoyed every minute of it. When I first began writing, I really wasn't sure what I was going to write. It didn't take me long to realize that romance would be my niche. I believe that every life deserves a little bit of romance, a little spice doesn't hurt either. When I am not writing, I enjoy the company of good friends and relaxing with a delicious glass of red wine.

I hope you found Ash enjoyable to read. Please consider taking the time to share your thoughts and leave a review on the on-line bookstore. It would make the difference in helping another reader decide to read this and my upcoming books in the Jagged Edge Series.

To get up–to-date information on when the next Jagged Edge Series will be released click on the following link http://allong6.wix.com/allongbooks and add your information to my mailing list. There is also something extra for you when you join.

Coming Soon!!!!!!

Gainer:Jagged Edge Series #6

Read all the books in the Jagged Edge Series

Hewitt: Jagged Edge Series #1
Cop: Jagged Edge Series #2
Hawk: Jagged Edge Series #3
Sly: Jagged Edge Series #4

Other books by A.L. Long

Shattered Innocence Trilogy

Next to Never: Shattered Innocence Trilogy
Next to Always: Shattered Innocence Trilogy, Book Two
Next to Forever: Shattered Innocence Trilogy, Book Three

To keep up with all the latest releases:

Twitter:

https://twitter.com/allong1963

Facebook:

http://www.facebook.com/ALLongbooks

Official Website:

http://www.allongbooks.com

Made in the USA
San Bernardino, CA
01 June 2017